Lock Down Publications and Ca$h
Presents

THA TAKEOVER

Written By
KEITH CHANDLER JR.

First Edition 2025

Printed in the United States of America

This is a work of fiction. Names, characters, places, and incidents either are products of the author's imagination or are used fictitiously. Any similarity to actual events or locales or persons, living or dead, is entirely coincidental.

Lock Down Publications
P.O. Box 944
Stockbridge, GA 30281
www.lockdownpublications.com

Like our page on Facebook: Lock Down Publications
www.facebook.com/lockdownpublications.ldp

Stay Connected with Us!

Text **LOCKDOWN** to 22828 to stay up-to-date with new releases, sneak peaks, contests and more…

Like our page on Facebook:
Lock Down Publications

Join Lock Down Publications/The New Era Reading Group

Visit our website:
www.lockdownpublications.com

Follow us on Instagram:
Lock Down Publications

Email Us: We want to hear from you!

Dedication

First and foremost, I would like to Thank God for giving me a new hustle so I would be able to feed my family.

This book is dedicated to my three beautiful daughters Jariah, Kai'Dynn and Ky'mora. Please remember that you all are my world and, as always, you all can turn to daddy for anything anytime y'all need me. I want you all three to know that I love y'all, so never forget it.

Acknowledgment

I have to thank all the people that believed in me and supported me when everybody counted me out. To all the people that wrote, sent pictures, money or took that ride to come up to see me. Thanks, I will always remember the love and time y'all put towards me.

Furthermore, I would like to thank my momma LaSonda and pops Big Keith for having me in 1989. Granny (Jacqueline), thank you for taking me in when I was just a young child, and grandma (Mattie), thank you for always accepting my calls and sending me love when I really need it. I love then both of my grandmas. Wylihsa (R.I.P), I would like to thank you for giving me my firstborn child. You will always be loved. Kymberlee, we have had our ups and downs but we made some good times too and I love you to death. Also, thank you for having my kids and always coming up to see me no matter what, and for making sure I had a relationship with my kids.

My brothers Curtis and Donnie, y'all are the most solid brothers anyone could ask for. Curt bra right on for standing up for me since you've been out and I want you to know I did this for us. Donnie, I think about you all the time bra and I really miss you (R.I.P.)

Shout outs: LaTalya, Desiree' and Amaya (sisters) even though y'all have not been showing it, I know y'all have love for y'all brother and I want y'all to know it's no hard feelings and keep doing y'all out there. Auntie Bugg, you are the best aunt ever and I will never stop telling you this, so get use to hearing it when we talk (Lick on the face) LOL. Ma-Ma (Jariah grandma) thank you for being a good grandma to my daughter. It really touched my heart over the years to see that you were the only one that stay in touch with me. Thomas (Tommy Gunz), Robert (Tezzy), Aaron (Lil E) and Mustafa (Scrill) y'all know y'all are my brothers and I will always have love for y'all no matter what. Marcus (Suce) you thought I forgot about you, but how can I when you forgot about me. You always broke bread with me ever since you started calling me James. Dustin, we grew up together and the love I have is a brotherly one so you will always break bread with me since you started calling me James. Dustin we grew up together and the love I have for you is a brotherly one so you will always be my brother from another mother. Your family is my family; we have a bond no other has my nigga. J.R bra, I want to thank you for the helping hand you gave while we were in the dorm; I can't wait to see your book out here so stop playing and get on your job ill nigga. Last, I would like to say to the ones that share my blood, just because we have the same blood doesn't mean we are family and since y'all haven't stood tall for me while I have been here, when y'all see me out there, act like y'all don't know me. Also, to them other haters, thank y'all because y'all are the ones that push the DAWG to sit down and write. To the whole WEST-SIDE of Indianapolis, y'all know We Da Best and we did it again. Not to forget my uncle Fred, Aunt Shante and a few cousins I didn't name but you know who you are.

Chapter 1

Accompanied by LR and Nasty, Uno walked into the warehouse on the Southside of Indianapolis to see his five head lieutenants. While walking to the head of the table, Uno looked every last man in the eye searching for any sign of weakness or fear. Knowing what he was about to say, he needed to be sure he didn't have any Judas sitting at his table. Content with what he saw, he began to speak.

"I called this meeting today, family, because it's time for a change. Any nigga that ain't part of this here family can no longer eat. Ain't no more passes— period." Everybody at the table just nodded knowing Uno was referring to Red and his people. Red was an outta town nigga who'd been in the city hustling for a few years. The OG's in the hood overlooked him hustling in the hood b-cuz he was hitting them off with a percentage every week.

Uno poured himself some Louis XIII and took a sip before continuing. His pause was calculated b-cuz he wanted his words to sink in while he read everybody's faces. "I'm the King of this city and I'm not called Uno for nothing. It's time for a takeover; we gone hit da nigga Red where it hurt the most and that's his pockets. Every street he has a house on, I want it shut down, ASAP. By the time it's over, I want him and his crew saying *they are greedy. They ain't letting us get no money*"

"Why don't you like Red?" Babyface asked Uno. Babyface was a lightskin pretty boy type that stayed fresh from his face down to his feet.

Uno took a sip of his drink and sat it back down, taking his time as usual before finally saying, "You see Babyface, it ain't that I don't like him, it's just that when you put two dogs in the same cage with one bowl of food, it's only a matter of time before the hungrier dog is tired of sharing. Feel me? " Again, everyone nodded. "Now." Uno began, "In order to accomplish this takeover, I need every one of you to let me know what you can handle. We have four parts of the city, so we gone have to split up and everyone has to hand pick their own crew.

Fat D, you'll take the south side since you have already been out this way with your people. Lil E, I need you to be West. Mo-Mo, you'll have to take the North side for me, and Babyface, you shoot out East. Since you have family out there, it shouldn't be hard to do; you feel me? Listen, I need at least two-three million coming from each section at least every two weeks. You will have to pay your crew yourself. It shouldn't be that hard to make that money after a few weeks b-cuz we are not taking anything less. I don't care if you have to make your workers and runners hug the block like we use to?

After everyone nodded, Lil E spoke up, which didn't surpass Uno because out of his whole team, he was the hungriest. Lil E was Chris Rock looking ass nigga. His saying is that he'll sleep when he dies.

Uno, whose name is Murrell Brandon, stood five-foot-eleven. He had deep brown skin and was 20lbs of solid chiseled muscle. His long black locs hung down to the middle of his back. Uno is the epitome of the word Boss.

Being brought into the world by a true soldier and raised and coached by two older brothers who were self-made and certified, it was in Uno's card to be that nigga. His head was made to wear that crown. With all the wisdom he got from his brothers through watching and listening paired with its natural hustle hand and street smarts. Uno ran the West Side like Boobie. Out of his genius was born the West Side Family. The man required to be put down with WSF was loyalty which Uno felt is what made pens family, rather than blood. From the beginning, Uno made sure that everybody knew what they were signing up for b-cuz disloyalty resulted in a closed casket.

Not wanting to live in his brother's shadows, Uno set out on his mission to prove to everybody that he was his own man that stands on his own ten toes. Now, here he was living lovely, doing everything he said he would and becoming the boss of the city.

"Well, I can handle at least twenty-five," Lil E said as he tugged at his goatee. On purpose, Lil E was put out west b-cuz if anyone could get a few million, it was him with a team backing him. "Okay, that is good, we got chu," Uno said smiling b-cuz he knew that none of his cliques liked to be outdone and Lil E's setting of the bar would only get higher he hoped. Uno turned his gaze in No-MO's direction and before he said anything, Mo-Mo spoke up. Mo-Mo knew Uno didn't want to hear any bullshit, so he wanted to impress him." Gimmie twenty-five of dem thangs until I see how the North is rocking but watch me make the friends go crazy out there" one thang for sure and two thangs for certain: Mo-Mo's wrist game was stupid and everybody knew it. Uno nodded before turning his attention to Baybface and saying, "And how are you going with my nigga?"

"It coo my way bra but that nigga Red dope is fire and he has better prices than we do" Babyface always kept it solid and never sugar coated shit. "So, if we gone shut shit down, we gone need some better work or our price have to beat that nigga shit, feel me? But let me get thirty-five tho."

Fat D chimed in "The south side is already rockin' like da 90's so I'll take twenty and twenty more. But Face is right, we need some good shit." Out of the whole clique, Fat D had a look in his eyes Uno couldn't point and he had the most kids.

"Lastly, Tezzy, how are you living Lil bro?" Uno asked.

"You know how I do, shoot first, ask questions last," Tezzy boasted. Tezzy was the smallest of the family, who had the heart of a lion and zero tolerance for bullshit. "As long as I'm in charge of the gun, we gon' take over the whole city with ease. I'm ready right now not to go out and get started," Tezzy said getting hyped at just the thought of putting in work for the family.

"Okay, I heard what you was saying, so after we flip these last birds, I'm gone have a talk with the plug on some better prices for us b-cuz I need this take over to go as smooth as possible; feel me, and I need everyone to do they part. Nasty and LR grabbed what everyone asked for; it's time to eat for real y'all," Uno said.

After everybody left Uno, Nasty and LR sat in one of the many offices they had talking and having a drink.

"So, we're really on this Take Over shit I see," Nasty said.

"Yeah, I want y'all to hit Red's blocks hard, I want them to understand my message loud and clear, I gotta get outta here, ' Uno said standing to his feet and looking at his Presidential.

"Well, me and LT gonna sit back and come up with a plan cause Red has the street I grew up on and I hate it," Nasty said leaning on his chair. Nasty looked like a skinny Rick Ross.

"Okay. Love y'all niggas and I'll get at y'all later," Uno said walking out the door.

"Bro!" hollered after Uno.

"What's good?" Uno asked, sticking his head back in the door.

"When you get home, tell Pooder I love her."

"Okay cool. I'll have her call you," Uno said, shutting the door.

Uno had a daughter by LR's sister and had known him and his family his whole life. When Uno started messing with his sister, LR knew he had gained a brother from another mother.

Uno loved riding in his F-150 b-cuz it always gave him a sense of dominance. Towering over every other car one thread and pressing on the gas never failed to feed his appetite for power. Uno bobbed his head to the Migo's new mix tape as he rode down MLK. Making a right on Roach Street, he pulled up in front of the blue double and jumped out.

"Uno! Uno! Uno!" A pack of little kids screamed, running up to him. Every kid on the block Uno frequented knew he always gave out money for candy and ice cream. Punkin stood off to the side smiling from ear to ear at how all the kids loved Uno.

"What are you smiling for?" Uno asked, walking up to get a hug.

"I'm smiling at how much the kids love you."

"All yea, you know what it is. But I love me some kids too, that's why I can't wait to put nine more in you," he said half joking."

"Whatever," she said, pushing his arm.

"Get your ass in the truck before you get into some trouble," he said slapping her butt.

"So, what's good?" she asked as she hopped up in the truck.

"What you mean what's good?" He looked at her crazy.

"Like I said, what's good, nigga?"

"Punkin, quit playing with me on the real,"

"If I don't stop, what will you do?" she asked, smiling. Her attitude and sassiness were two things that made her attractive to Uno.

"Aw, now you a gangster, I see," he said.

"Shid, you made me this way nigga."

While shaking his head at the truthfulness of her last statement, he couldn't help but smile. Before they started messing around, Punkin was a good girl for the most part. Standing five-foot-five in was light skin beauty with a smile that could take a man's breath away. Pretty, book smart, and independent Punkin was everyday dope man's dream girl but before she had blossomed, Uno had seen the potential in her and cuffed her up. Ever since Uno popped her cherry, she'd been madly in love with him. The things he did to her body had her dickmatized in the worst way. Uno had her mind, body and soul.

Chapter 2

"Punkin, come up outta them clothes, you were on some gangster shit with me in the car a few hours ago, but now you are acting like you are scared of this here dick; it's not going to hurt you too bad," Uno said smiling at her. It was time Uno felt Punkin wud do shit to make him shitty, so he'd fuck the shit outta her.

Smiling back seductively, she knew he wanted her badly by the look in his eyes. "I'm not scared of anything. I'm a big girl, I can handle anything that comes my way, feel me," she said looking him in the eyes as he would know she wasn't playing. For a moment, Uno didn't respond. The more he molded her deeper, the more he fell in love with her. She was down for whatever when it comes to Uno and she was blessed to be able to call her his woman b-cuz most women weren't willing go that extra mile to please their men. Knowing her better than she knew herself, Uno knew she had something on her mind b-cuz she was still standing in front of him stalling on taking her clothes off. Finally, Uno spoke.

"What's on your mind baby?" He asked, leaning up on his elbow.

"Well, since you asked, I want you to listen to everything I have to say before you give me an answer please baby," she said poking her lip out.

"Ok cool, hit me with whatever you have Punkin."

13

"You know what type of woman I am, I'm an independent woman that likes to stand on her own ten toes as you know, but at this moment, I don't feel independent because I haven't brought anything to the table, so if it's ok with you, I would like to start doing my share."

"So, what do you want to do?" Uno asked.

"I want the same thing you have, baby?" Punkin said.

"What do I have that you don't?" He asked looking her in the eyes. "For starters, you have power and respect. I want that and more. Secondly, I feel like I would be some type of help with the WSF. I'm already in the middle of everything and everybody already knows me. I know it's something I would do to help this family build. You are the KING and I'm the QUEEN and I want everyone to start acting like it. I'm tired of being called Uno's girlfriend. I'm much more than that."

"I tell you what...Uno briefly paused in thought, willing to give Punkin anything she wants with the quickness. Uno was hesitant to subject his queen to the dirty game he played every day since he was 12, even tho she had been around it all her life. I understand everything you just said, and I want you to know you do bring a lot to the table, so don't ever feel like you don't." Uno said.

"What do I bring to the table, Uno?"

"You bring love and happiness to this family and that's a lot." "Punkin's groan melted Uno and he gave in. "But I will give you Roach Street. You should be able to handle that with no problems. All you have to do is control runners, workers and the money. You are already a Boss, so bossing people around should come easy to you since you had been doing that to me for years," Uno said smiling."

"Shut up boy! You're crazy," she said, smiling back." "Now since you are a female, a lot of people won't take you for real, so you have to hold it down and turn your heart cold while you are out there in the streets. It's niggas that's going to let you do you because me, LR, and Dustin but it's niggas

14

out there that don't give two fucks who you are or who you under, feel me?" Uno said meaning every word.

"If anybody tried their best, I believe I will handle mine. I learned from the best and you know I keep that 22 you gave me for my sixteen birthday a few years back. But how will the person you have in charge now take it that I'm comin' in to replace them?" She asked.

"I'm the boss, I do as I feel is best for this family but if you don't want to take it, then fuck it."

"No I want it," she said as she turned around and looked back while taking; off her shirt. Next came her skinny jeans with only a bra on. She unhooked it now standing in front of him naked."

"Uno looked at her skating his head because she was so beautiful. Getting in bed, Punkin went to the top of Uno's lap and rode his dick through the night."

"Man-Man, I'm tellin' you my thug, niggaz got us fuk'd up, thinking they gon' get away with this shit." Big Head was all riled upland; it sounded like he was practically yelling into the phone." Man-Man could imagine Big Head's big black linebacker build ass spazzin' as spit flew outta his mouth.

Big Head's name came straight from his mother at birth. She was scared and pushed for what seemed like an eternity, so she felt the nickname was only right for him.

"These WSF niggaz must think we some bitches or sunning," Big Head commented." Talkin about how they can get currency anywhere they want and ain't a mu'fucka gone stop "em"

Man-Man blood boiled as he listened to his man's spill. WSF was fuckin' up the game, doing two things he hated to do most; starting trouble and disrupting the cash flow.

"Okay listen" Man-Man finally said. 'Who exactly was it that hit da block?" He asked.

"Tha ill homies said it was Tezzy, Nasty, and LR" Big Head informed. Man-Man shook his head at the mention of the names. Tezzy was the straight menace out of them all and automatically lessened the odds of this shit getting handled without bloodshed or making him look bad.

"Aight, tell the thugs to be ready but to stay put. There must be a misunderstanding" Man-man said ending the call. He could've sworn he heard Big Head suck his teeth before he'd hung up but quickly dismissed the thought as he hurried and dialed another number. While the phone rang, he stepped inside Double 8 Foods on 29th Street.

"What's good Man-Man?" Red asked.

"Check dig OG. The WSF niggaz must be trippin' hard cause some of 'em came on the block causin' static."

Red was a tall light skin, green-eyed, slick-talking cat from New Jersey. He came to Nap ten years ago with kilos for sale and a dream and never looked back.

"Listen," Red told Man-Man "You're my under boss, so you need a handle that." His voice stayed in its usual laid back tone. "I'm busy right now, so gon' handle that and get at me later on." Red finished before leaving Man-Man listening to the dial tone.

Walking to his BMW Man-Man jumped in and navigated the luxury car beeping the horn at the people he knew as he headed the block. He shook his head at his precarious situation. He expects Red to make an OG call, not tell him to handle that, but handling that is exactly what he planned on doing one way or the other. As Man-Man hit the block, he saw a lot of new faces posted up. Knowing where the new faces belonged to, he grabbed his 9mm at his stash spot, after hitting redial on his phone, he told Big Head, "come outside" and hung up. Parking behind a money-green Jag, he saw Big Head walking off the porch. Getting out of his whip, he began walking toward the cocky LeBron James lookin' nigga he knew to be L.R…….. Even though the WSF was surrounding him, Red's order was fresh on his mind. LR looked up and saw Man-Man approaching. The taller but significantly thinner Man-Man was dressed in all white topped off with a fresh fade.

"What's happening? LR got down, and he really didn't have the heart to be a part of any beef with the public enemy number one. Yet, being surrounded by his clique, Man-Man couldn't show any sign of fear, so he poked his chest out and played his role. He was a boss too and had a whole crew of young wolves, so he had to demonstrate that he was standing on something or lose their respect. "What you mean what's happening niggah?" LR shot, looking him up and down.

"Don't you know who the fuck block this is mu'fucka? Y'all must gotta death wish."'Man-------Man started. Watching LR"s eyes turn black, Man-Man knew he had fucked up by talking recklessly to him. LR hit Man-Man with a two-piece that knocked him out cold. Only lighting could've struck faster than LR hands.

"Daayyum," a WSF worker marveled "his gold came out". Before Man-Man's clique could respond, they are surrounded by LR shooters. LR stood over Man-Man kicking him until he finally came to out from his little nap. Looking at all the guns aimed at him and his clique, Man-Man thought it was over. Lil Chris, one of Man-Man's people, stepped forward in an attempt to help the big homie up.

"Stop right where da fuck you are" Tezzy commanded, pointing his pistol at the side of Lil Chris' head. Lil Chris turned to look Tezzy directly in his eyes, no fear present. Everyone knew how the short light skin nigga from Post Road got down; how he'd have nigga stinking n a heartbeat but Lil Chris didn't give two fuck' bout none of that.

"Man, that gun don't scare me nigga, they ain't stop making them when you got chorus" Lil Chris spat.

"You right" Lil Tezzy said. Bak! Bak!

"Get your bitch made azz up Man-Man." LR instructed, not at all fazed by the dead body that rested a few feet away from him." I want you to gon' tell yo' pussy azz boss his time is up and that these blocks are WSF blocks. Now nigga, you got 60 seconds to get da fuck out of my face. Jumping up Man-Man didn't waste any time getting to his car and burning rubber leaving smoke.

Later on that night, LR stepped out of his house he had in the 3rd. Walking to his car, he never even saw the shadow on the side of the house waiting on him.

"You thought it was over," LR heard, and as soon as he turned around, a bullet struck him in his shoulder. The impact from the bullet almost knocked him down but he caught his balance and stumbled behind a car for cover. LR ups his 9mm off his hip but balanced himself and stumbled behind a car for cover. LR ups his 9mm to his hip but before he returned fire, the night grew quiet and still again. "Damn!" LR hugged, feeling the burning pain in his shoulder. These pussy ass niggaz had the balls to try and kill me?!" The comment was just as much of a statement as it was a question. Fuk this, it's on one. Speeding down 31st, LR said a prayer. "GOD forgive them for their sins, for they know not what they do. And forgive me, for the sins I am about to commit amen."

Chapter 3

LR woke up from a bad dream he knew all too well. It had been years since he'd had one and he thought they were gone for good. Getting out of bed to go take a piss and get himself together too quickly caused an excruciating pain to shoot through his arm. "Fuk!" he grimaced. Grabbing his toothbrush and brushing his teeth before jumping in the shower. Standing under the soothing water, LR thought back on his life until his dream popped back up.

4 Years Earlier

LR stood in the back of a house on 29th MLK making a sting. While putting his dope back in the duck off, he heard a gun cocking back.

"Nigga, you know what it is, grab that dope and gimme the bread out your pocket too" LR heard a voice behind him bark. As LR dug his hand back in the spot and while searching for the dope, his hand ran across this knife he kept in there. Wrapping his hand around the handle, LR turned around rapidly fast stabbing the gunman in the throat. Dropping the gun, the gunman grabbed his throat; his eyes got the size of golf balls. LR picked up the dude's gun and let two shots off into his chest. Uno came running from the front with an AK-47 with the nuts hanging in his hand.

"What the fuck happened?" Uno asked, but LR was unable to speak. Uno grabbed the gun out of LR's shaking hand and picked up the knife as he pushed LR towards the car.

"Nasty" Uno shouted. "I need you to call the cleanup crew and tell them to hurry up and get here and clear that shit up in the back ." That was LR's first murder and out of all the murders he'd committed or ordered since that one was the one that haunted him. He dint know if it was b-cuz it was his first one or what. LR's ringing phone burns him back to the real world. Getting out of the shower, he walked into his bedroom to grab the phone. Looking to see who was calling, he saw it was his sister's picture on the screen.

"Hello," LR said, sitting on the bed.

"LR, why the hell you didn't call me to let me know you were coo," Punkin asked. Knowing how his sister was, LR said "Sorry sis."

"What's good with you and Pooder? Y'all need anything" LR asked her.

"Naw, I'm good and as you know, Uno takes good care of Pooder" Punkin said into the phone.

"Well, I'm still going to drop some money on her when I come through.

"Ok, fine with me, but the girl doesn't need shit but a good ass beating. She is too damn grown up and it doesn't make any sense" Punkin said looking at Pooder. LR knew his niece was a handful with Uno and Punkin's blood runs through her.

"You better not be over there hitting my niece tho', and if I find out, I'm going to fuck you up," LR said.

"Boy, whatever, I have been beating your ass since we were kids," she said and they both started laughing." But listen, the street has been talking about you getting shot and Uno is shitty. You need to get low for a few days." Punkin paused. "You all I have besides Uno and Pooder, so you have to be coo. Please, she said crying.

"Ok, Ok sis, I promise to take it slow, so stop all that crying," LR said..

"So, what do you have planned for your soul day this year bro cause it's approaching in the next few months?" Punkin asked.

"Shid, I really don't know, maybe I'll let you and Uno put something together for me. Since it's my 21st birthday, you know I have to show out for the hood" he said meaning every word.

" Well, we have time. I have to go. Love you bro," Punkin said.

"Ok, I love you   too and tell Pooder I said hello." LR hung up the phone and lay back on his bed and just thought about what his sister said about everything. Over just a few years, Uno had helped him to get his bankroll all the way up. And still, it was only the beginning. By the time he turned 25, he was looking forward to the life of a young millionaire.

Red walked back and forth in the basement of a house that was located on the Far East side. He was clutchin' twin .45's which only added to the fear of his soldiers. Before now, most of the men in the room had never had to deal with Red personally and it was obvious that the Boss was pissed the fuck off. Standing in front of his soldiers, Red was shitty.

"Now who had control over Indianapolis and Pairs Street," Red asked.

"I did," a fat black dude named Jake said."

"So tell me, how do you let them come and take over our blocks without a fight?

"How the fuck you let them come and take food out of your family mouth," Red asked, shooting off questions towards Jake while making eye contact." "come up here to the front."

Walking slowly and nervously through the aisle, Jake eventually made it to where Red was standing in front of the whole team.

"Now, tell me how you let them take the blocks," Red asked.

"They...They pulled up from everywhere at the same time and we didn't have a chance to do anything. Red stood behind Jake and raised his gun firing two shoots into his head.

"You see, I don't want to have to kill any of my own people, but before I let a mu'fucka take out of my mouth, I will kill all y'all." Red paused to let his words sink in before continuing. "We are at war right now, so either you goin' be ten toes down or you ain't." Red pointed to the stairs; if anyone of you needs to feel it's too much, there is the door, go now."

Everybody in the room knew any nigga that chose to leave would get bodied, so they all stayed as still as tombstones.

Red proceeded. "Okay then, y'all don't let that type of shit happen again. If it does, then you might as well kill yo' got damn self. Feel me? Now get the fuck up out of here before I get hotter" Red said, sitting down before downing a glass of Remy.

Meanwhile, across town, Uno took more blocks from Red. "If it's going to be this easy taking blocks from these niggas, we'll have shit sewed up in no time" LR stated.

"You know" Uno said just like me LR, Red is not a bitch. He is an older player in the game and he will not just sit back and let us keep takin' shit from him, so it's a matter of time before he shows his ass. Feel me? So we need to be ready. I want watchers on every corner with walkie-talkies so this way we can all talk to each other in all four parts. If they'd come through, they won't have time to get out the hood without us getting back at them." Uno knew exactly what was to come and he wanted to make sure LR and the rest of the FAM" were on their p's and q's and did not underestimate Red and his crew. He wanted to make it through this war with very few casualties.

Chapter 4

Punkin was born and raised in Indianapolis, Indiana. Growing up in the hood Punkin had it just like everyone else. Being from the hood dubbed "LAND LIFE" or "DA LAND" for short, Punkin continued to have it hard until the age of 15 when she and Uno started messing around.

Knowing Uno all her life, she didn't think she would be able to talk to him 'cause she'd despised him so much since they were kids. Uno would always pick on her for having big ears and she hated that.

In the beginning, Punkin had only told LR about her and Uno's relationship and that was she going to be moving in with him very soon? So, on the weekend, she and Uno pulled up in a truck. LR already knew what was up but a lot of her family didn't know what was happening until they started moving her stuff.

Punkin's mother didn't care that much but being that both sides of her family were from the same hood, a lot of them did have something to say. Some of her people just hated that she was moving into her own crib at a young age. Some of them wish they were in her shoes and some of them were happy to see her come up. Punkin could care less what anybody thought, she was gone regardless.

10 Years Earlier
When Uno walked in Punkin's mom's front door, music was blasting and Punkin was in the middle of the floor

dancing to "Pretty Rick", a group that was hot at the time. Uno watched how the sun dress he wore moved with her body.

Turning around, Punkin saw Uno lookin' at her.

"What are you lookin' at?" Punkin asked with her nose up in the air. Knowing they couldn't stand each other, Uno took a chance and walked up on her and grabbed her lookin' her directly in the eye.

Punkin tried to shake out of Uno's hold but he was too strong.

"Listen, I want you, and I know in the past we had our problems but something in me wants you bad," Uno said before kissing her. At first, she tried to back away from him but eventually ended up melting in his arms. From that day on, Punkin knew she belonged to one man and that was Uno.

"Bitch, I have told you many times before that I'm not talkin' any shorts," Punkin screamed, standing all up into a female face. "I can't take half my money to the light company and ask to bring the rest back later, can I?" The frightened woman shook her head no.

"Now you can go get my money, or let one of the homies get it another way, and we don't have all day, so you need to make your mind up before it gets ugly in here bitch." Punkin had taken to the game like a duck to water and she wasn't playin' games. She was goin' hard on niggaz and bitches. Plus it didn't help if she didn't like you in the first place.

The girl Punkin was hollering at this pretty chocolate girl with long silky black hair that came all the way down to her ass. Her name was Amber but everyone called her Mix Breed 'cause they thought she was mixed with something. With everyone lovin' her beauty, she let it get into her head, walking around with her nose up in the air thinking she was better than everyone in the path.

Mix Breed was a tall woman, her long thick, sexy legs resembling those of a coffee-colored more. After getting in trouble while going to a township school, her parents decided it was best to send her to stay with her grandparents.

Punkin had met Mix Breed at Washington High School where they had a few classes together. On the first day Mix Breed got beaten up, Punkin had started it because she stayed buttered in all the top-of-the-line clothes. To Punkin, the bitch Mix breed walked around like she owned the whole world. Even tho Punkin had started fresh, she still didn't like Mix Breed.

Back in those days, crack had just hit the city and had everyone stealing from their loved ones. One night at a party, they are playin' 'truth or dare' and one of Punkin's friends double dared Mix breed to try a blunt laced with crack. Motivated by a burning desire to fit in, Mix Breed tried a blunt laced with crack. Motivated by a burning desire to fit in, Mix Breed smoked the laced blunt, hoping it would get her into the 'n crowd.'

From neglecting her perfect hair, her flawless chocolate skin decayed right before her peer's eyes. She didn't care about herself let alone what her once entourage thought. She was only concerned about getting her next high. She went from skin;' laced blunts only to now sucking on a glass dick.

Even tho Punkin was happy that Mix Breed wasn't that bad bitch anymore, she still wasn't satisfied.

"Well, bitch what you going to do? I told you I didn't have all damn day," Punkin said standing in front of Mix Breed smiling.

"Punkin please don't do this to me. I promise I will have your money soon" Mix Breed pleaded."

"Bitch listen to me, either you got my money now or you going to fuck for this good dope I have. So what's it going to be? If you don't tryna get high, then kick rocks 'cause you've already wasted a lot of my air." Punkin said, getting mad.

'Ok, Mix Breed finally said. "What do I have to do?" She asked looking down at the ground.

Punkin turned around, looked at all the people in the house and asked them what they wanted to do. Pumpkin's gaze fell on a skinny brown-skinned dude with big ears named Mo-Mo, who was grinning and shaking his head. He was trippin' off how Punkin fitted right in as a Boss bitch.

"What are you over there smiling for Mo-Mo? You tryna fuck dis slut?" Punkin asked, desperately wanting to humiliate Mix Breed.

"Nah, I'm good. You better pass that bitch to one of dem runners. Shid, I gotta sign on my dick anyway and da' mu'fucka says bad bitchez only" Mo-Mo said before busting out laughing at his own punchline and walking off.

Punkin couldn't help but crack a smile at Mo-Mo's arrogant ass before continuing her search for a *jiggalo*. Punkin asked people if they wanted to fuck Mix Breed while she stood there feeling small. It was so hard for her to just stand there and accept this but she wanted that high bad.

"Shid, how about you Nasty?" Punkin asked. Nasty was a Boss nigga but everyone who knew him knew he didn't turn down no pussy.

"Nah, I'm good Punkin," Nasty said. Nasty knew how deep Punkin's hate for Mix Breed ran and he wished he could save her right at the moment. Mix Breed had always been cool back in the day when they were in school but since Punkin was the Boss of this spot, he fell back until he could holler at her alone one on one away from her workers and runners.

"What's good y'all?" Mike asked as he and Two Black walked in the front door.

"Shit trying to get someone to fuck this bitch" Punkin said pointing all in Mix Breed's face.

"Why? What's wrong with her?" Two Black asked, looking at Mix Breed like he was the big bad wolf.

"She just trying to get some dope but don't have enough money for it, so she has to fuck for it. Punkin said smiling."

"I'm down. You?" Two Black asked his partner. Miek and Two Black didn't know the hatred Punkin had for Mix Breed cause they were a few years older and they wanted to be part of the WSF.

"Well, what are you standing there for bitch? Handle your business. Come on outta them clothes and show my niggas a good time and if they are pleased with you, I will throw you a little extra." Go grab the cam recorder Punkin told one of the runners.

"I'm putting this shit on tape and selling them for $19.95 each."

"Let Me holler at you for a minute Punkin," Nasty said, walking off to the side so they could have a little privacy. "Yo, you over here trippin' hard Punkin on the real. I'm not going to tell you how to run your spot but, you need to get it together 'cause if LR and Uno come through and see this hit, they will shut this bitch down. Nasty chided. Really, you are showing these little niggas it's cool to trick off our dope but I guess b-cuz at the end of the day, as long as when we count up our number, they are right," Nasty said before walking out of the house. Punkin strolled back into the room that had turned into XXX set. Mix Breed was deep throating Two Black dick, while Mike long stroked her from the back. In spite of the fact that Punkin was ecstatic that she'd gotten Mix Breed, she was shitty at how Nasty checked her.

Chapter 5

Ant pulled his escalade to a slow crawl before stopping in front of two trees that sat side by side in the distance. The sight of them caused a melancholy expression to shroud his face, his absence clarified by how much they'd grown. Ant sat simmering as he always did before he visited his Big Brother.

His mind wandered back to when times were still lovely before he was left with no choice but to take the leading role in the family before he was ten toes in the streets and on his way to the NBA where he was prophesied to become the next A.I. of his time.

But that was all before the hood threw him a curveball that ended up getting him in a little trouble and sent away for a while. After serving a few months, Ant returned to the streets and said *fuck sports and the nigga who made them.* Picking up a gun and a sack, Ant dived head first into the streets with no snorkel.

Though he was the smart laid back brother of the bunch who had so much potential, so much promise to do something special, the streets ended up having a different plan for his life. As the wind blew across Ant's face, he thought back to when his life changed for the second time in his life.

Few Years Earlier (The Night Omar Died)
Ant, Omar and Ron stood on Udell talking for the last twenty minutes before Ant had to head home to his girl. As

Ant pulled away from the block and was about to jump on the highway, he heard a few shots ring off but he didn't think anything of it because being from the hood, you heard shots all the time, so he didn't pay them any mind. About ten minutes into Ant's ride home, his phone started blowing up like crazy and since he was on his way home, he didn't want to pick it up thinking it was someone trying to grab some dope. A few minutes later, Ant was walking in the front door of the apartment he shared with his girl.

"How are you doing baby?" Lauran said, getting up to hug Ant as he took off his shoes. "You hungry? I cooked tacos tonight," Lauran said.

"Naw baby, I'm good. All I'm trying to do is chill. I will eat later on, thank you anyway" Ant said, sitting down in his lazy body so he could relax.

Ant owed his relationship with Lauren to one of Uno's ex's. A few years back, he'd asked Uno ex's to hook him up with one of her home girls but she had to be a solid female. So she quickly turned him on to her best friend she grew up with. Ant and Lauran have been going strong ever since.

As soon as Ant was comfortable in his chair, his phone started ringing again, but this time, it was his mother's ring tone.

"What's up mo-" Ant's voice trailed off? For a few seconds, he just listened to the cryin' and screaming coming from his phone, uneasiness creeping into his heart.

"Momma, momma, slow down, I can't understand what you are saying" Ant stated, getting up out of his chair. His chest is tightening up as he heard and felt his mother's pain, through her bawling.

"Ant, they shot your brother" he heard her wail through her cryin'. Ant immediately grabbed his keys and headed to the door.

"Lauren, something bad happened, I have to go see what's up," he said before walking out.

"Seeing the look on Ant's face, Lauran knew whatever it was, was deep, so she ran out the door to go with him."

Hitting 80 on the highway, Ant realized that he didn't know where he was headed to.

"Baby, I need you to call my granny for me to see what's going on and where they are please, thank you," Ant said, handing her his phone.

"After a few minutes on the phone, Lauran started cryin' because she knew when she told Ant the news, he was going to see red. She hung up the phone and just looked at Ant for a minute to get her thoughts together."

"Baby, I'm sorry to have to be the one to tell you but they shot your brother Omar up. Your family is at the hospital."

"What?! No! Not big bro," Ant yelled thinking back to when he heard the shots go off before getting on the highway earlier. They had to be connected, he thought."

"Speeding up to 100 mph towards the nearest hospital to the hood, Ant kept wondering if he would have stayed a little longer could he have saved his brother from getting shot. As they reached the hospital, Ant and Lauran saw the family outside grieving and praying for Omar."

"When Ant walked into the hospital, the doctor was coming out from the back with a look on her face, which Ant knew too well."

" Hello, my name is Doctor Jones, are you all in the family of Omar Chandler?'

"Yea we are," Ant said, stepping up. "That's my brother."

"I hate to be the one to have to tell you but unfortunately, Omar did not make it sir," Doctor Jones said, giving Ant a sympathetic look. At that moment, all you could hear was crying throughout the entire hospital lobby."

"Omar passed on April 29, 2006, and after his death, their lives were never the same."

"Snapping back to reality, Ant kissed Omar's tombstone and looked up to the sky. He could still feel the pain in the place where his heart was broken that gruesome night."

"I love you big bro and yea, I came to town to look after Uno's crazy ass" He still thinks he's slick," Ant said. He took a deep breath and stood there for a minute before finally walking away.

Over the Keith Sweat song, all you could hear in the entire house was Punkin moaning as Uno slipped his tongue in and out of her pussy."

"Umm, baby, eat this pussy" Punkin moaned as she spread her laps open so that Uno's tongue could go deeper. Takin' Punkin's clit in his mouth, Uno could've easily made her cum, but he didn't want it to end just yet. He began kissing his way up her body until they were face-to-face and she grabbed his face kissing his lips, tasting her own juice."

"Not wanting to be outdone, Punkin flipped Uno on his back and took him into her mouth, inch by inch. Uno looked Punkin in the eye and could tell that she was enjoying herself by the way she was sucking and moaning. Uno grabbed a hand full of Punkin's hair and started fucking her mouth like it was a pussy."

"Damn baby, you got that good head" Uno moaned, lifting his body up off the bed so Punkin could get his whole dick."

"As she started to suck faster, she felt Uno's nut rising."

"Make this dick bust baby," Uno moaned. Seconds later, he explored in her mouth and she fell next to him where they held each other until they fell asleep.

"Uno was awakened by a loud noise downstairs. Grabbing his .357, he headed down to see what the hell was going on, but as he hit the hallway, his nostrils came in contact with the smell of pancakes, eggs, and apple oatmeal. When he bent the corner, he saw Punkin in the kitchen doing her thing with the help of his daughter. He just stood there to take in the moment before turning around and headed back up to the room to jump in the shower and get his day started."

"Stepping in the shower, the warm water relaxed his body and mind. Rubbing himself with a new body wash, he made sure he got cleaned before he stepped out of the shower and was rushed by his smiling daughter.

"Daddy, Daddy, I cooked for you," Pooder said, dancing around him as she signed his name."

"What, you did, all by yourself?" Uno asked while playing with her.

"No daddy, you know momma helped me."

"Pooder! Uno!" Punkin called from downstairs. "Y'all need to get down here and eat before y'all food gets cold."

"Go keep momma happy while I get dressed," Uno said kissing his daughter.

"Also, your uncle LR said he loves you," Uno told her as she walked out the room.

Chapter 6

"Word got back to me who the nigga is that shot you was," Tezzy said to LR as they chilled in the spot."

"Who is he? LR asked, making himself a drink."

"His name is MD; he's one of Red's shooters. I know this bitch that he messed with tho. She gave me the nigga's address and everything. You want me to handle 'em?

"Nah, it's good, I'm going to handle this myself ill bro, and LR said smiling." Red just killed MD and he doesn't even know it? LR said.

"Shid, you tryin' to handle this because I'm down for the cause, Tezzy said."

"The sooner the better," LR said ending the conversation so he could answer his phone."

"MD sat in his apartment playing X-Box that he had just purchased.

"Damn, Red needs to come on with some more work, I need some bread bad and I'm trying to shoot someone with this new 9mm I just got," MD said to himself. He was the kind of shooter that took his job seriously. Having power over someone's life made MD's dick rock hard.

"What are you out here doing baby?" Jessica asked, coming out of the kitchen from cooking dinner. Once she saw her man playing his game with his 9mm in his hand, she already knew what he was on that night. She was still just as amazed as she was when she first met him at how such a handsome dude could be so evil."

"Jessica and MD have been tighter for 10 years since they were 20 years old. No matter what MD did, Jessica loved him more than she loves herself as her mother told her how a woman was supposed to be."

"Baby, we haven't done anything in so long, can we go to the movies or something? Please?" Jessica asked, sitting down next to him."

"I can't tonight baby, I have to go out and bust a few movies for us" he said, standing up.

"I LOVE YOU" she said, standing to kiss him on the lips."

"You know I'm a good shooter," Tezzy said to LR. "But this dude MD is older and good at what he does, so we have to be on point."

"You know I don't give two fucks about any of that, he over with," LR said grabbing his two .45's out of the stash spot."

"Tezzy pulled up on the block a few houses down from where they were headed and killed the engine."

"You ready?" Tezzy asked.

"You already know," LR answered as he slid out of the car."

"As LR and Tezzy walked down the block, MD was coming out of the house."

"A Yo, that's the nigga right there," Tezzy said, tapping LR on the arm."

"MD saw LR and immediately knew who he was. He tried to run back into the house but it was too late."

"LR sent six shots in MD's direction. Three shots hit MD in the back spinning him back around. By the time he'd spun in a full 360°, his 9mm was already out.

"LR and Tezzy ducked behind a parked car in front of the house MD came out of. MD dropped to his knees because of the pain shooting through his body."

"Listen, we have to get this nigga before the copes show the fuck up," LR said, "so you take that side, and I'll go this way."

"Ready, Ready," they both said. LR ran from the side of the car and ran up on MD. Lying on his side, MD looked up and saw LR standing over him."

"I knew when I didn't kill you that I would be dead soon. LR let two shots off in MD's head and he and Tezzy ran off to the car."

The WSF had a house on 34th in Clifton where they sold crack and whatever else they had their hands in. The landlord of the house was an OG named Lee that grew up in the 3rd, so everyone knew everyone that was from the hood as well.

OG LEE knew Omar before he got killed, so when Uno came to him about renting some houses, he welcomed him with open arms and they came up with an agreement. OG Lee owned a few houses that the WSF sold dope out of.

Standing five-nine with light brown skin, OG Lee rocked a bald head and looked like Mr. Universe. OG Lee had done 13plus years in prison for a murder he didn't do and with his time, he had worked out, played basketball, and got his mind right. He made a promise to himself never to walk back into another prison and when he got out, his brother blessed him with his Lawn care business and signed over two houses he owned. OG Lee never looked back once his foot hit the soil. Now, a few years larger, OG Lee has one of the biggest lawn care businesses in Indianapolis and thrown over ten houses just in the hood, not counting the ones on 34th watching how all the dope heads filled in and out the spot like it was a McDonald's joint.

"Man, let's go in and get something to drink. It's hot then a bitch out here" Lil E said, walking towards the house. When they all walked inside, they saw Mix Breed on the floor high as a kite.

" Damn, this bitch is high as hell. I'm about to get myself some of that pussy" Mo-Mo said, walking towards her while

Lil E and Fat-D went to the back of the house. Even tho MO-Mo had seen some nasty shit done to her, he still wanted it just to say he fucked her but he didn't want anyone to know."

"Pulling his pants down, Mo-Mo began to beat his meat till it was standing straight up. Grabbing Mix Breed roughly by the waist, MO-Mo pulled her into his dick."

"Not being aroused because her pussy wasn't wet, she felt an intense pain shoot through her body. It wasn't until then that she realized that Mo-Mo had slid inside her, the high she had was instantly blown by the size of Mo-Mo.

"Take it out! It hurts!" Mix Breed screamed."

"Running from the back of the house, Lil E and Fat-D saw Mo-Mo fuckin' a screaming Mix Breed from the back.

"Man, what the fuck is wrong with you?" Lil E yelled.

"Ignoring her screams and Lil E, Mo-Mo kept pushing in and out with his eyes closed."

"Shut up bitch and take this dick. Mo-Mo was enjoying this cause back in the day when they were in school, Mix Breed didn't even give him the time of the day. Because Mo-Mo didn't have money and was ugly, he couldn't get any play from her, but now that the tables had turned, he was going to treat her like the whore she was."

Mix Breed was in so much pain; all she could do was take it and scream. Looking down, Mo-Mo saw he had blood all over his dick.

"You stupid bitch! Why didn't you say you were bleeding?"

"Lil E and Fat-D pointed at Mo-Mo and laughed. Mix Breed just curled up in the middle of the floor cause she didn't want Mo-Mo to start beating her.

"Get up out of here Mix Breed" Lil E said handing her her clothes and a wad of money."

"Nasty walked in the house to see a naked Mix Breed standing in the middle of the floor."

"What's going on here?" Nasty asked.

"After Lil E explained everything, Nasty just shook his head at a now-thinking Mo-Mo."

"Back when they all were in school, Mix Breed and Nasty had a few classes together and they'd worked on a paper together, so he knew she wasn't all that bad like everyone said."

As Mix Breed got to the door, Nasty yelled, "Hey Mix Breed, take my number. If you ever want to get yourself together, call me and I will get you some help. Make sure you get yourself some food with that money Lil E gave you and tell one of them, youngsters, to give you a gram so you don't have to spend that on dope."

"Thank y'all so much she said, putting her head down."

"Man, look at this save ho" Mo-Mo said walking back into the room to see Nasty helping Mix Breed out."

"Bro, the bitch bleeds on me and you going to give her dope and you give her money?, he said looking from Nasty to Lil E. "Y'all tripping?" Mo-Mo said.

"Listen nigga, did nobody tell you to go sticking your dick in a crack head raw. You need to be glad we did that for her cause if she goes to the police, we could be charged for rape."

"You aren't lying." Fat D said. "Let that bitch have that shit, it ain't nothing." Mo-Mo was about to say something but his phone started ringing."

"Hello? Who this?" Mo-Mo asked into the phone.

"Nigga it's Uno, who are you with?"

"Nasty, Lil E and Fat-D. We all in the 3rd chilling, Mo-Mo told him, firing up a breezy."

"Well, Baby-Face should be pulling up to grab that dust from you in a second. And tell them other two niggas the same thing will be happening to them later once they are at the spot. It's about time for me to go holler at the plug."

"Is that the WSF nigga's right there?" Two-Tall asked Big Head as they pulled up on 34th Street."

"Yeah, that's them," Big Head answered, surely, I bet Red wished he was here," said Big Head, pulling his Lexus over to the curb. Sliding out of the car, he made his way over to the circle of dudes followed by Two-Tall."

"Yo, my man, who is the boss of this block?" asked Two-Tall.

"Me, why and who wants to know?" The worker responded with his chest out, looking at Two-Tall and Big Head like they were crazy."

"Listen, I heard your block is getting a lot of money, and with that being said, y'all need to get off of it, Red want it," Big Head said.

"Nigga, this is a WSF block, so you need to fall back and count your blessing that you are not dead for stepping on this block talking about Red bitch ass," he said giving dap to his people.

"Listen, either get off the block or else little nigga." Big Head said getting mad by the second b-cuz this youngster didn't know he was a born killer."

"This is our block, I'm not going anywhere."

"So I'm going to give you a second chance to walk away with your life, the worker said."

"Ok, so bet it," Big Head said and he and Two-Tall walked off jumping in their car. Big Head grabbed the AK-47 with Da 100 round drum from the back seat. Two-Tall pulled off slowly while Big Head hung out the window and let the AK-47 sing like John Legend."

"Everybody tried to run or hit the ground. By the time they hit the corner, 90% of the block was laid out on the ground."

"Did y'all hear them shots?" Lil E asked running out of the house with his 9mm in hand. Running behind him, Fat-D and Nasty also came out of the house brandishing pistols. When they looked down the block, all the workers were laid on the ground. It looked like a scene straight out of a movie.

"Let's get out of here and go handle that business," Nasty said walking towards his car as he heard the police get closer."

Chapter 7

"It's about time you made some time for me," Tiffany said as she sat down in a chair.

"Shit, been busy a lot," Red said as he relaxed in his house in Fishers, Indiana.

"Tiffany was the woman who stayed down the street from Red. She was a middle-aged white woman that always had a thing for black men but never did get with one until Red moved down the block from her. She was a housewife with no children at home."

"Baby, come give me a back rub," Tiffany asked, setting her wine down on the table and lying on the floor.

"Man, why are you always trying to get a brother to work?" Red asked playfully. Ten minutes into the back rub, Red heard his business phone going off.

"Why is someone calling me while I'm with you?" Red said grabbing his phone seeing that it was a text.

"Boss, me and Big Head went through 34th street and killed a lot of WSF dudes, so we fell back for a few days." Red read before shutting his phone off and getting back to giving Tiffany a massage.

"Baby, is everything ok, who was it?" Tiffany asked.

"Nobody," Red answered. Red rubbed the side of her breast and started licking her neck."

"Rolling over on her back, Tiffany grabbed Red by the neck and started kissing his lips while he reached down and played with her pussy."

"Mmm, baby that feels good" Tiffany moaned as she bit on her lip." I love the way you make me so wet," she said.

"I want to taste that pussy" Red whispered. Red made her get up and take off her clothes and sit on the edge of the chair and spread her legs. As soon as he was face to face with her pussy, he put her legs on the handle of the chair. Red planted kisses all over her pussy and clit.

"Ah Red," Tiffany moaned as her body squirmed in pleasure. Seconds later, she started grinding her pussy on his face while pulling him in more. From the way she was moaning and squirming, Red knew she was about to cum, and cum she did all in Red's mouth. Tiffany tried to run from his horary tongue game.

"Standing up before taking off his pants, Red stood in front of Tiffany while she tried to regain her composure. With his dick in Tiffany's face, she grabbed it and put the whole thing in her mouth.

"Damn," Red moaned, grabbing Tiffany's hair as he looked down into her eyes. The way she was sucking and moaning it only took him another three minutes for him to nut all in her mouth.

"Damn, this white bitch can match my sex game," Red thought.

"Listen, it's some of them WSF niggas on 25th and we need that block, so get them up out of there ASAP. They don't mean shit to Uno b-cuz they are just worker, so there's no reason to call the hit men for this job feel me." Man-Man said to Big Head and Two-Tall.

"This shit is so easy bro, like taking candy from a baby," Big Head said. Big Head and Two-Tall were first cousins that liked putting in work. Big Head got his name 'cause his head was so big. Standing five feet tall and black as hell, Big Head always tried his best to dress and get money b-cuz he knew women wouldn't turn down his money even if he was ugly.

"Two-Tall was six feet four, brown-skinned and rocked a box cut. He use to play basketball back in the day until he broke his leg which left him with two options and he couldn't rap, so he chose the gun and hit the streets full throttle.

"When Big Head pulled up on the block, the two young niggas that were standing out there had it popping like it was the 90s. The two were grinding all in the open like they had no care in the world.

"Yo, I'm going to keep these nigga's still while you open them up but keep one alive so he can give our message to Uno," Big Head said pulling up directly in front of them. Jumping out, Big Head had a gun out and on them

"Y'all better not try to run," He said pointing his 9mm at them.

"Man, what's this all about?" One of the kids asked, looking down at the ground.

"Shut up," Big Head said hitting him with two shotted heads silencing him forever. The other kid was shaking like a snitch at a gangsta party and pissing on himself as he stood there looking at his homie brains spilled out on the pavement."

"Please don't kill me man. I was trying to get a little money."

"Damn, this little nigga pissed on himself," Two-Tall said hitting him with a three-piece to the jaw." Tell your boss he better stop grinding on this block; Red owns this bitch now."

Jimmy sat behind his desk in his back office, watching as Uno and LR pulled up to my shit," Jimmy said to his bodyguard and best friend Music.

"Let me go open this door for these bitches," Music said, walking towards the front of the house. "Gentlemen," Music spoke, opening the door with his SK held tight in his hand.

"Music what's up with you?" Uno said as he and LR walked into the mansion.

"Jimmy is in the back office waiting on y'all," Music said in an unfriendly tone. As LR walked past Music, he gave him an ice-cold stare. LR didn't like Music; it was just something about him that LR couldn't quite put his finger on yet, but he'd surely keep his eyes on him.

"What's good with y'all?" Jimmy asked standing, giving Uno and LR pounds.

"Listen, I need you to drop them prices on the bricks," Uno said getting straight to the point, "we grabbing a lot of them."

"No can do. As a matter of fact, I need to put a little extra on what you are playing now," Jimmy said leaning back in his chair. It's a temporary thing; shit is a little fucked up for me right now, but if you stick with me, I promise to show love later," Jimmy said to Uno.

"Shid, we are not willing to pay extra b-cuz then, we will be losing," Uno said looking at him crazy. You can raise them prices on them niggas, but I'm a boss nigga, you can't get me like that. I cop more than 500 bricks every time and you want me to pay more?" Uno asked, shaking his head. "I have a lot of people to feed, so you need to come up with something better, and to top it off, the work I have been copping is good, but it's stepped all on. Now you want more?"

"Ok, same price for you Uno," Jimmy said.

Standing up, Uno looked at Jimmy: "In a month, I want some new shit and new price b-cuz if I keep getting the same shit, I ain't telling what's going to happen," Uno said before he and LR walked out.

"Boss, why are you trying to beat Uno? He spent money with you" Music asked, not sure of Jimmy's method.

"Fuck that young bitch, he thinks he is a beast," Jimmy said looking at his monitors on the wall.' He should be glad I even fuck with him b-cuz I don't respect these young dudes in the game right now. They are all silly if you ask me. See, he's at war but still trying to sell the most dope in the city. You can't make money and have a war; it doesn't make sense. Feel me?" Jimmy said. "And if he keeps talking to me like that, I'm goin' to cut him off."

"What if he finds a better connection with better prices, then where will that put us b-cuz he does bring us a lot of money," Music said looking at Jimmy.

"Find a new connect where?" Jimmy questioned, laughing. I've been beating Uno for years, if he was going to leave, then he would have been gone. He is not smart like that.

"Why the fuck are we still paying the same price for the same work, we suppose to get a better deal right?" LR asked confused about the meeting.

"When his people bring the shipment, we are not going to pay them for the work nigga," Uno said stopping at a stop sign.

"You know that's going to start yet another war, we are going to need help with that when that starts," LR stated.

"That's the plan that just popped in my mind. You know I will come up with something better, but I'm not worried about another war bro. My gun is going to bust. I'm going to take it back to the old days and put this work in and show these youngsters how a boss moves. Really, I was playing b-cuz Red should have been dead. Feel me? Let's end this shit with him here in the next few days if we can." Uno said.

"You know I'm down for whatever," LR said.

As Uno pulled up on Udell to grab some loud from one of their spots, his phone rang out.

"Hello, what's good Nasty? Uno said into the phone.

"Shit chillin' bro, but that nigga Red sent his people to come through 34th and 25th and sprayed it up over the last few days. We need to do something about this ASAP," Nasty said.

"Ok, we are going to let the workers, runners and bosses have a little fun these next few days so they can relax their minds and then we are going to go hard to end this shit," Uno said hanging up. Shitty Uno hit the steel wheel and looked at LR, "the nigga got 25th and 34th, it's really time to quit bullshitting and dragging our feet. "Let's turn up the heat," Uno said.

Chapter 8

A few days later, Uno stood on Udell in front of a house smoking a blunt. To everyone, it looked like he was all by himself but he had two shooters posted in the bushes watching his every move. As he was lost in his thoughts, a black Roll Royce Phantom on 24" auto couture rims pulled up. Being in the hood, the car was out of place.

"Let me holla at you Lil Bro," Ant said from inside the car. Uno hopped in and gave his brother love!

"What good?" Ant asked, looking at Uno's face.

"Man, this is a nice car bro, but should I be chilling, trying to keep my head up?" Uno replied passing the blunt to Ant.

"Listen, I 've been in town for a few days and I've been putting something together, feel me?" I know you need a new connect because the one you have now isn't playing the game fair." Ant said.

"How do you know about my business? Uno asked, surprised that Ant knew so much about his business.

Ant was the smart laid back one out of the brothers but don't take that smart laid back role to be soft cause he was deadly with his.

Standing five feet nine, brown skin, 208 lbs, with dreads, one would call him a lady's man. Neither he nor his brothers was ugly but Ant had a baby face that the ladies loved so much and he knew that, so he had all the women loving the ground he walked on.

Uno knew his brother was trying to blow his question off. "Anthony, why do I get the feeling you are not trying to answer me ugly ass nigga? Uno asked smiling. B-cuz he knew his Big bro hated when people used his government name."

Ant laughed but not because of the obvious reason. His laughter came from seeing how far his ill bro had to come in the game. The game had changed him a lot over the years for the good.

"Naw, it's nothing like that ill bro. I was just thinking of a way to help you out. Now I know some players out in MIA, but they have nothing to play with. So, if you want, I can set it up for you to go out and meet them," Ant said.

"Hell yea," Uno said smiling. "But you know I have a little war going on right now", Uno said, his smile fading away. But it ain't nothing I can't handle when I get back," Uno told Ant.

"Yeah, get that war over with ASAP and if you need me to, I can call some shooters, just let me know."

Pulling up to that building" Uno said to LR, pointing to a four-story Brownstone.

"Listen, I'm going to take the nigga in, then a few minutes, you and Nasty come in guns blazing," Uno instructed before getting out of the car. As Uno walked up to the building, he saw the person he was looking for.

"My nigga Roy, what's good?" Uno asked.

"Shit, you tell me my nigga," Roy shot back at him."

"Same shit, trying to get money," Uno said. "Listen, Jimmy told me to come and grab that from you," Uno said in his laid-back voice.

"That nigga never called and told me that," Roy said. "Let me give him a call to see what's up," Roy said pulling his phone out of his pocket.

"Drop the phone," Uno said, placing his 9mm to the side of Roy's head, "or I drop you."

"Damn, it's like this? I thought you were better than this," Roy said. "Jimmy ain't going to let this go when he finds out" Roy laughed, hoping to discourage Uno and save his life.

"Fuck Jimmy, I always handle any problems I have in life," Uno said leading Roy to the stairs. "Y'all still keep that work in the back?" Uno asked.

"I'm not giving you shit nigga. Fuck you! Just kill me now," Roy said, thinking if he could get to the gun he had in the back or not but then LR and Nasty walked into the building.

"What's good bro?" LR asked, toting an AK-47 while Nasty held two357s.

"This nigga wants to be a tough guy," Uno said before letting two shots off in Roy's head. "We have to go grab that work from the back," Uno said, stepping over Roy's body. Uno killing Jimmy's cousin, sent a message to him and Red's crew that he wasn't playing with them anymore.

For the last hour, Uno and Punkin lay in the bed mixing business and pleasure.

"Damn baby, you look so stressed out," Punkin stated looking into Uno's face. I know the war is weighing heavy on you but you can't let it get to you. You have to end it and definitely fast. You can't let Red regroup and get stronger than you. You need to go home with all you have because we are losing a lot of runners and workers. Better yet baby, you need to just put some money on his head and watch all these young niggas' guns for it. Shit, even some of his own team will after hearing the fat as price tag, feels me?" Punkin said meaning every word and not liking that Uno looked stressed out."

"Yea, that's a good idea," Uno admitted, liking the new version of Punkin more and more, "and with Ant benign in town, he'll give me an even stronger team." Getting up and kissing Punkin, Uno walked to the door. "We are going out tonight," he said before walking out.

"I love you baby," Punkin hollered behind him.

"I love you too," Uno said sticking his head back in.

Chapter 9

LIL E, NASTY, MO-MO, TEZZY and BABY-FACE all pulled up to Ant's and Uno's club. Aunt Bugg's back to back in their toys busting ass.

"Damn bro and OG have this club looking good and it's jumping in there, Lil E said as they all gave each other a dap."

"Come on let's get up in there," Nasty said tucking his gun in his waistline, before leading the way.

"What's good, my nigga?' Nasty said, giving the bouncer a pound while slipping ten, fifty dollar bills in his hand.

"How many did you get with you tonight? The bouncer asked Nasty.

"It's just us five right here," Nasty said pointing to everyone.

The club was in full swing as they walked through the door. All you heard was Jim Jones.

"We fly high no lie you know this ballin'."

I saw some real ballers just walking in the building. "WSF what's happening?" The DJ shouts out. Tezzy was only twenty, so he never went to this type of club. Looking around, Tezzy saw all types of people running up to Nasty trying to get dap. Even though he was from out POST, he was connected with WSF because of Uno. As they walked through the club, they saw LR waving them over and pointing to the office that overlooked the whole club. When they made it up to the office, they saw Uno had his own party going.

"My niggas, glad y'all could make it," Uno said giving everyone a dap.

"Shid, we had to get out the hood, shit is crazy," Tezzy said walking over to the table Punkin was sitting at drinking.

"Listen, like I told everybody else, tonight is about having fun, but tomorrow, we get back serious," Uno said. I think I have some info on Red's people, I just have to check it out. I'm down playing games and Tezzy, you never got back to me about some of his houses," Uno said.

"Damn bro, I forgot all about that with this war going on. My mind has been somewhere else."

"Well, right now, everyone just enjoy the rest of y'all night; it's time to play, so go hit the dance floor and get some pussy," Uno said walking to the window that was the dance floor and slid it open and began to throw money out of it making it rain on the whole club.

This war had the streets of Indianapolis going crazy and the squad almost forgot how much fun it was to just hit the da club and turn up. Around 3 am, the club was letting out, so Uno and the rest of WSF walked out a little tipsy but still on point.

As they stood in front of the club waiting for their cars, a car came zooming around the corner with a dude hanging out the window.

"Watch out, it's a hit," LR yelled dropping to the ground.

Ducking down, Nasty, Tezzy and Lil E all pulled out their guns but they were too late as bullets started raining at the front of the club. Jumping off the ground, all three of them started running after the car, letting their pistols bark. One of the shots hit the gunman and as the car took off down the street, the gunman's lifeless body just hung freely out of the window.

"Is everyone coo?" LR asked getting up from the ground."

"Naw, I'm hit Lil Bro," Uno said, rolling off Punkin's back and this bitch hurts badly as hell."

Punkin jumped up screaming. "Noooo, baby don't do this to me! Please!" She said now crying.

LR shook his head as he looked at his man and saw the blood on his shirt.

"Fuck! I'm going to kill those bitches," LR said while dialing 911.

Mo-Mo, Nasty and Lil E helped Uno sit up a little. As they moved, more blood came gushing out of Uno's open wound.

"Punkin put some pressure on the wound so it would stop bleeding until the police got here," Mo-Mo said.

"Baby, stop crying, I'm ok," Uno said.

"We're at club Aunt Bugg's" My brother had been shot.

"Baby-Face dead too." Tezzy chimed, walking up to LR.

"And we have a body out here," LR told the 911 operator. LR ends the call and looked Uno in the eye. "We have to get out of here y'all LR said looking around at his people but Punkin you need to stay here with bro."

"Count that bread up," Uno said to LR before he left."

LR just shook his head b-cuz even though Uno was on the ground bleeding, his mind was still on the money.

Uno and Punkin marveled as he lay there on the cold hard ground and all the pig's wanted to do is ask a sleuth of questions.

These mf's must've lost they fuckin' minds, Punkin thought. "Hold up. Here my man is on the ground bleeding the fuck out and all you wanna do is fuckin' ask questions? Y'all mf's tripping out here," Punkin screamed.

The cops were surprised that she dared to raise her voice the way she had. The white cop face said that they could care less if the black man lying at his feet died or not.

After Punkin finished spazzin' on the cops, they backed away so the paramedics could do their job.

"Is my man going to be ok?" Punkin asked the EMS.

"Yes. He will be fine" One of them answered.

"I'm riding with my man," Punkin said as she jumped into the ambulance.

The next day, Uno sat in the hospital bed flipping through the channels trying to find something to watch. The only thing on T.V. was the news and they were talking about him getting shot and Baby-Face getting killed.

The Police Chief was promising to lock up every gang member that walked the streets of Indianapolis so he could make them safe again. Crime was at an all-time high b-cuz of the killings and drug deals.

God was with Uno cause the bullet went in and out. Uno looked up at the open door and wasn't at all surprised at the two detectives that walked in.

"How are you doing?" Mr. Murrell Brandon?"

"I'm chilling. What y'all want?" Uno asked, sitting up in the bed.

"Do you know who shot you last night?" The black detective asked, holding a pen and pad ready to take notes.

"Naw, all I know is I was standing outside the club and shots were fired, Uno responded.

There wasn't anything else the detectives wanted to ask him. The white detective gave his partner a look that said Uno was full of shit.

"Well, if you remember anything else, here's my card, cause the next time you might not be able to help us get the prep who shot you. He spat as they turned and walked out the door.

"That roach knows more than what he was telling us. Did you see his eye?" the black detective asked his partner.

"Fuck it; it makes our job easy at the end of the day.

Uno picked up the phone to call Ant to let him know he was coo and would be home soon.

Chapter 10

A few days later, LR and Nasty were sitting in one of their Avon stash houses. Nasty and LR sat with blunts between their lips and piles of money all around them. The scene looked like one straight outta a gangsta movie.

"Bro, we gotta be on point at all times just in case this nigga Jimmy finds out it was us that got him. And on top of that, we can't let that shit that went down at Aunt Bugg's happen again," Nasty vented.

"Right now, we are good all around," LR said, exhaling a thick cloud of kush smoke.

"And niggah, you know I stay on point."

Being older than LR, Nasty always saw to it that he dropped wisdom on his Lil Homie. He knew LR was tired and true but he also knew that it didn't really matter if a nigga caught you slippin'.

"Yeah, I gotta go grab Uno after this, he is ready, "LR added, wrapping a rubber band around a stack of money.

"Aight, make sure you tell the goons to be strapped up 2nite to b-cuz we gotta go handle that shit with Red, it can't wait any longer." Nasty said while putting all the money into the third duffle bag.

"How much did it come up to?" LR quizzed.

"4.5 million and 450 bricks of uncut. Nasty said." "Damn, LR said shaking his head."

LR and Uno walked in the front door of Uno's four-bedroom house to see Punkin and Pooder lounging on the sofa watching their "72" inch flat screen. Happy to see Uno, both girls jumped up and ran straight into his arms and began to kiss all over his face. As Uno hugged them, back pain shot through his body, but he didn't stress it cause he was home with his two girls.

"Baby, why didn't you call me to pick you up?" Punkin asked.

"LR was already there, so I left with him, Uno said with a smile."

"Releasing her grip from around his neck, Punkin let Pooder target her moment with her daddy. Her heart warmed as she watched the two of them.

"What's up ill bro?" Punkin asked, turning to face LR.

Looking at her, shock overcame him. The fact that his sister was a trap Queen was still hard for him to get used to.

"Shid, chilling outside, you good?" LR asked back.

"Yea, I'm good. Glad baby is home." She said looking at Uno and Pooder playing on the floor.

"Baby, would you fix me and LR something to eat?" Uno asked. "And make something good too. Please.

"Punkin nodded before she headed for the kitchen." Pooder, you want to help me fix your daddy and uncle something to eat?" Punkin asked, getting up off the floor. Pooder looked at Punkin, "I have to give my uncle LR a hug and kiss first," she said, running into LR's arms.

"I love you uncle LR," Pooder said.

"Aw, I love you too baby," LR said putting her down "Here," he said handing her a roll of money.

"Thank you," Pooder said running towards the kitchen to show her mother what her uncle LR had just given her.

Uno and LR took their seats on the sofa, glad to be home and out of the streets cause it had been hot. Uno thought 20 minutes passed before Punkin and Pooder emerged from the kitchen carrying two plates.

"Here y'all go," Punkin said, handing them their plates."

"Mmm, Miss Punkin, thank you," Uno joked.

"Whatever nigga, do y'all want anything else?" she asked standing in front of them with her hand on her hip.

"Ummmm, Naw Miss Punkin, you've just about done enough for right now," Uno said winking his eye.

"Listen bro, Ant is supposed to meet up with you so y'all can go grab something for the funeral. I also got some info on one of Man-Man's hoes, so we went on that tonight. Plus, we are trying to get this war over with Big Bro but I gotta get up outta here. I need to handle a few things, and make sure everything is good for tonight, feel me?" LR said finishing his food and standing up. "Are you good?" LR asked seeing the big homie's demeanor change.

"Yeah, just stay low key b-cuz I don't want to lose you my nigga. Just put Mo-Mo and Tezzy on it, they are good at handling their business, feel me?" Uno said looking up at LR.

"Ok, I'll play the background until you hit the streets again. I also have that money for you and the other money from the four parts. We are looking real good," LR said with a smile.

"Do you have our lawyers on standby? Just in case anything goes wrong!" Uno asked knowing LR stayed on point.

"We are good on all that bro", he assures. Well, let me go grab this money so I can be on my way," LR said walking out of the door.

Moments later, LR stepped into the door and dropped two bags on the floor "Love y'all," he said before shutting the door.

Uno sat on the sofa and watched TV until Pooder fell asleep in his arms. Carrying her up to her bed, Uno laid her down gently enough not to disturb her. Uno's heart was warmed as he took a few moments to watch his little angle before cracking the door and leaving. Back on the sofa, Uno heard his phone ringing, "Baby, where did you put my phone when you left the hospital?" Uno asked, walking towards the ringing.

"Look in the room on your side of the bed," Punkin yelled.

"It's crazy Uno hasn't called to get his shipment. My bones are telling me that he had something to do with my spot getting hit Jimmy said."

"So how do you want to go about this shit, Bossman?" Music asked, ready for whatever.

"I'm not sure yet, first I have to see if it was him or somebody else. I'm about to call him right now, hand me my phone off the desk." Dialing Uno's number, Jimmy waited until he picked up.

"What's good? This Jimmy," he said in a laid-back voice. Being able to read a nigga came easy to Jimmy almost like a sense or sunning

"I see your name on the screen, so I know who this is, what's up? Uno asked.

"Yo, somebody marked Roy and took some dope and money from the spot, so I was calling to see if you knew anything about it since you run these streets," Jimmy said.

"Naw, really I've been chilling out lately," Uno said shortly. He never took the rope Jimmy was giving him to hang herself.

"I can't imagine anyone who has a big enough set of balls. Nor whose head is empty enough to pull some shit like dis on me," Jimmy stated really shooting shots, trying to see if he could get Uno to bust back and give himself away.

"Yeah, I don't know who did it, but whoever pulled a move like this had to be smart and sending you a message, Uno said."

"Well, if you hear anything, make sure you get at me ASAP," Jimmy said in a threatening voice.

"I got you," Uno replied, hanging the phone up.

Jimmy looked at the phone and saw red from the disrespect he just got from Uno. Jimmy was no dummy; he knew Uno at least had something to do with it.

"It was Uno and his people" Jimmy finally admitted to Music. Jimmy hadn't said anything to Music about how short Uno was b-cuz at first, as much as he felt it, he didn't want to believe Uno had a hand in the ordeal.

Man-Man sat in his crib watching VH1 when his phone started ringing.

"What's up? Man-Man said into his people.

"I need to see you," Red said before hanging up the phone. Man-Man walked up to Red's club that sat on the far east side of town.

"Glad you got here so fast," Red said, sipping his drink.

"Yo, I need you, Ride and Black to handle something important," Red said, looking Man-Man in the eye.

"What do you need done?" Man-Man asked.

"I need y'all to grab Punkin up for me. Get to her, we get to Uno. Red said.

"Say no more, we're on it," Black said standing up.

"Man-Man gone show y'all who she is, they all use to go to school together.

Chapter 11

The Gucci store located on the third floor of the Circle Centre Mall in downtown Indianapolis was well known for its stylish quality, and one-of-a-kind clothing.

The store owners were this middle-aged couple, Jane and Chan. They opened the store after they had their second child a few years back. The store only carried top-of-the-line clothes, so if you didn't have top-of-the-line money, it would only be a waste of your time to even walk inside the store.

Ant opened the door and walked into the store followed by Uno. The clerk behind the desk knowing Ant and Uno were big spenders hit the button under her desk to let her Boss know that someone important had come in.

Chan seeing the red light in his office going off, immediately made his way to the front of the store to see who it was. Seeing two of his biggest spenders, he walked up to them wearing a warm smile.

"My guy Chan?" Ant said, holding his hand out for him to shake.

"What's up Ant?" Chan greeted, taking hold of Ant's hand.

"What's up, Chan?" How are you my friend," Uno said, giving him a handshake also.

"Everything is everything," Chan responded. "So, what are y'all here to shop for today, my friend?" Chan asked.

"Well, we're going to a funeral, and I need the best when I bury my man, feel me?" Uno said.

Babyface was WSF and Uno wouldn't dare let him see his final resting place in nothing but the best.

"Come to the back, I got just the thing," Chan said walking off towards the back. In the back, Chan opened a door, and inside were suits and loafers.

Ant walked up and picked up a pair of loafers smelling their freshness and running his fingers across the texture. Ant looked at Chan and smiled.

"I want these in all the colors, with the suits to match."

"Tallying up the bill fast, Chan smiled back cause he knew he was about to rake in a small fortune.

"Let me get these loafers here, and these four suits," Uno said pointing at four different colors of loafers.

As Chan was about to say something, the red light went off again.

"Sorry, I will be right back," Chan said.

Uno and Ant just shook their heads at Chan.

"Bro, after this funeral, I will be ready to hit MIA. I just got done with what I had" Uno said. I also need you to help. I need you to holler at your connects and find me and address on Red b-cuz he becoming a real fucking headache" Uno said looking at his brother.

"Listen, you just worry about this meeting this plug. I will get you the address." Ant said, looking at some more boots.

"Hello, welcome to my business. May I help you," Chan asked, looking from the guards at the door to the man sitting in the chair."

"Yes, you can help me. Can you please tell Uno I need to speak with him please?"

Turning around on his heels, Chan walked back to the room Uno was in.

"Uno, there's some Mexican cat out there asking to speak with you. You can look on my monitors and see who he is" Chan said walking into his office.

Uno saw Jimmy standing casually at the clothes, Uno immediately went to see what he wanted with Ant right behind him.

"What's up? Why are you asking for me" Uno asked, walking up to Jimmy.

"I just saw you come in, so I wanted to stop in to see why you haven't come to re-up, I'm waiting on you," Jimmy said.

"I'm good right now, I'll holler when I'm ready for you, and if that's all you wanted, then let me get back to what I was doing. Uno and Ant turned around and walked to the counter where their clothes were waiting on them.

When it was all said and done, Ant's bill was $25,385.00 and Uno's was $9,247.00 and that's cause Chan showed them love.

The entire church was filled with people coming to show their respect and to lay one of the WSF soldiers to rest. Sitting in the front row was LR, Uno, Punkin, Nasty, and Ant. On the second row sat Mo-Mo, Fat-D, Tezzy and Lil E.

"Young brothers and Young sisters, today, we are here to celebrate the life of one of our brothers that was gunned down in these dirty streets. Today, I had my sermon all planned out, but the Lord has led me in a totally different direction and I hope y'all don't get mad at me about that. Can I get an amen?

"Amen pastor," the church yelled.

"We need to come together as a community, so we can stop all these killings and the drug slang.

"Amen! Preach!" shouted an old lady.

"At the rate you, young people are going, the funeral homes are going to be full" The crowd stood up and clapped.

As LR sat there listening to the preacher talk, all he could do was think of revenge. After service, the whole WSF rode through the city for Babyface one last time with them stopping out west.

Chapter 12

Red and Man-Man sat in TGI Friday eating in the back. As they ate, they never saw the pair of eyes that had been watching them for the last hour from the bar.

As they continued talking, someone sat down and both men looked up to see a Mexican in a fresh suit.

"Jimmy," he called, extending his hand.

"Who the fucks are you?" Red asked, reaching for his hip."

"Listen Red, don't go getting ahead of yourself. I'm only here to talk with you about a problem you've been having."

"How do you know my name" Red wanted to know.

"You see, I'm not the police and I understand this might seem crazy but I know a lot about you. Jimmy said.

"Ok, what business do you have with me?" Red asked, sipping his drink and looking Jimmy in the eye.

"Basically, I'm about to make you an offer you can't refuse," Jimmy stated.

"I'm listening, go ahead," Red said still looking at Jimmy.

"It's like this, I know you are at war with Uno. I used to be Uno's connect but I feel he robbed me because he hasn't been to re-up and plus only a few knew about that spot. Uno was grabbing a lot of work from me and without him on my team, I will be losing. I have mad work but I need someone to move it for me. I have runners, and workers, I just need someone in the streets. I was thinking since Uno doesn't have me to hit him off, he will fall and at the same time you getting work and what's yours, the streets," Jimmy said.

"Shit, sounds really good, but I have my own plug," Red said.

"Ok, think about this, Jimmy said getting up from the table. I will give you each a brick for $12,000 and it's good to work here," he said sliding a bag under the table, "and here's my number, get at me when you are done with that," Jimmy said walking off.

Jumping in his Range Rover, Man-Man pulled off down the block with Black riding shotgun. The duo bopped their heads to 50 Cent as the luxury vehicle glided down the pothole-infested streets unaffected.

Black played with his pistol for the entire ride getting ready to do what he does best-put work.

Twenty minutes later, Man-Man pulled up across the street from one of Punkin's spots.

"Aight, look, as soon as the bitch is by herself, we gon' get her," Black said. Not two seconds later, they spotted Punkin walking towards the car.

"Damn, that bitch is sexy," Back said, undressing her with his eye. I think we should grab her at one of those lights," Black said.

"Shut the fuck up bro, you are tripping hard," Man-Man said following Punkin.

"Yeah, this Uno nigga must be getting a little money," Black said looking at the Lexus truck Punkin was driving."

"Yea the nigga and his team have been moving bricks. I know all of them from when we all were younger" Man-Man said.

Ten minutes later Man-Man watched Punkin pull up into the driveway of a white average Brownstone house with a wrap-around porch screen on it.

"I'm goin' to pull up and grab the bitch. But you have to be quick Man-Man said, pulling up behind Punkin's truck. Black immediately hopped out and sprung into action.

Punkin pulled into the driveway of one of her crackhead's house and let the engine die. The only thing on her mind was getting to the money and then making it home so she could lie down. She bent down to grab the dope from under the seat. Just as she was about to get out of the car, she saw a black Range Rover pull up blocking her in. Punkin panicked knowing Uno and LR were at war. She quickly snatched the 9mm Uno gave her days ago from its spot.

Black hopped out of the truck and tried to open Punkin's door but she let off two shots into the window making him take steps back and duck for cover.

Making it out of the car, Punkin let a few more shots off towards where Black was and connected with his chest, sending him crashing into the car. Turning her aim towards Man-Man, she let her gun bark like a dog while she back peddled.

Punkin ran in between houses being carried by pure adrenaline until she got to the Family Dollar store.

The fact that the store was crawling with customers did a lot to pacify her trepidation. Never had Punkin been subjected to the ugliest facet of the game she was now having second thoughts about being a part of. And her queasy stomach as a result of her thinking of the man she'd shot possibly being dead, only made matters worse.

Hiding out inside the store, Punkin called Uno's cell twice, but didn't get any answer. Dismayed Punkin tapped her foot while she clutched her phone tightly with trembling hands. She tried to remember where he was, then it hit her that he was over his female friend Alexi's house.

"Baby are you ok? You were screaming you are sorry in your sleep," Alexis said getting up from the bed. LR didn't want to look at her. "Did you hear me, LR? Are you ok?" she asked again.

"Yea, I'm good," he said heading to the shower.

When he walked back into the room ten minutes later, water was dripping from his body and his towel was wrapped around his waist. His clothes were folded on the bed and there was a plate of food on the table. He got dressed and started digging into his plate.

As he was finishing his food, Alexis walked in looking beautiful as always. Alexis was five-foot-one Mexican with long dark brown, ass-length hair. Her high cheekbones and dimples gave her a look of pure innocence that attracted LR but her mysterious eyes are what kept him mesmerized and in her clutches for all of three years now.

"LR, I want to say I love you, and that if you need me for anything, I'm here for you anytime," Alexis said, "and your phone was ringing while you were in the shower."

Grabbing his phone he saw two missed calls from Punkin. He died her number right back.

"Hello, what's up Punkin?" LR asked into the phone.

"Bro, that nigga Man-Man and some black ass dude tried to get me, but I shot my way out of the car and ran," Punkin said voice cracking.

Hopping up, LR ran out of the house and jumped up in his BMW truck.

"Where you at now? I'm on my way to you" LR said.

"I'm at Family Dollars on 30th out east," Punkin responded.

"Ok, I'm there in ten minutes; don't move," LR told her before hanging up.

Pulling up in the parking lot of Family Dollars with smoking tires, LR looked around for Punkin.

Punkin came running out of the store and hopped into the car looking scared.

"Where is Uno,?" LR asked. "I tried to call him so many times and he still hasn't picked up or called back," replied Punkin, apparently mad.

"Bro and Ant went out of town to handle some business for us this afternoon; they will be back in a day or so, but when he hears this, he'll for sure be on the first thang smoking home.

"These niggas got us fucked up, this shit just got a whole lot deeper now. Dis shit is personal now, it's time to call a meeting and I want you there. Someone will be with you at all times b-cuz this should never happen. LR said.

Chapter 13

Ant and Uno looked around in amazement at the sight of the tall palm trees, women walking around in two-piece bikinis of all sorts, the expansive breathtaking ocean view, and foreign cars that were zooming through the streets. This was the first time Uno had been down to MIA, but Ant had been there many times, but the sight was still a beautiful one to him.

"Looks good, doesn't it?" Ant asked looking at how Uno's face was, portraying his awe. "Come on bra, you are acting like you haven't been to any place beautiful before," Ant said, still looking around while walking to the waiting car.

As they drove through the city, they saw pimps, prostitutes, and even crackheads smoking out in the open on the corners. No doubt about it, there is no place on earth like MIA, not even Indianapolis.

"Bro, you get that info for me yet, cause the city is getting hot b-cuz of this war," Uno said turning his phone on.

"Yeah, I got that for you and as soon as we are done with this meeting, we can handle that," Ant said sitting back.

Ant and Uno met up with Fred and his bodyguard downtown in a magnificent restaurant that Fred owned. Fred shut down the whole restaurant for this meeting, so when Uno and Ant walked in, he knew who they were.

"Welcome to the MIA," Fred said holding his hand out for a shake. Dressed in a gray three-piece Metallic Floral Suit, Fred definitely looked like a check.

"Gentlemen, have seat" Fred offered and they all sat. "Do y'all want anything to drink?" Fred asked.

"Naw, we good," Uno spoke for both of them.

"Well, let's get this over with. I heard y'all need a little help with a connect since y'all stopped dealing with y'all old one," Fred started looking at Uno and Ant.

"It's not us. My brother isn't in the game anymore, feel me? He still has connections I don't have, so he set this meeting up for me. I'm the one that needs the connect b-cuz the work I was getting was like 6 in half to a 7 and I was paying way too much for a 6 in half. I'm a Boss, so everything I do needs to scream Boss. Feel me? I need some work that would shut down everybody's house in the city making them come to cop from me. Also, if we can get a deal made tonight, I promise you, it will always be nothing but good business on my end," Uno said looking Fred in the eyes to let him know he meant business"

"My people told me Ant was a good solid dude, so on that, I'm going to mess with you. I have some dope that's like 85% pure, so you can step on that like the rest of these dudes around here do and it will still be good," Fred said.

"Now, I want to know how you would get it back to your city, if you don't mind me asking," Fred asked.

"Listen, no disrespect to you Fred, but that's none of your business and the only thing you need to worry about is counting all this money you are about to have rolling in unencountered."

"He just doesn't know he passed the test," Fred thought as he shook his head. "Well, you talking about good," Fred said, shaking Uno's hand.

When it was all said and done, a deal was made and Uno left out feeling like a new man.

Uno's phone started ringing as they hopped in the car. Seeing it was LR, he picked up immediately.

"Hello, how is the business?" LR asked, referring to the plug.

"Shid, everything is all love," Uno said letting him know they secured the plug and money was about to fly in.

"Listen tho, we need you back in the city like tonight," LR said.

"Is everything coo? I will be back in the A.M." Uno told him, trying to see more of MIA."

" Bro, they almost touched Punkin today," LR said knowing Uno would paint the city red when he gets back."

"What happened, Uno asked, looking at his watch?" After Uno listened to everything, he just hung up the phone.

"They tried to touch Punkin today," Uno said to Ant as he watched the city pass. I have to get back ASAP tho, feel me?"

"Let's get back to the city, I'm glad I packed myself some Timberland boots. Let's end this shit with Red so you can take the streets," Ant said.

"Take us to the airport," Uno told the driver."

"Listen y'all, the Queen of the city almost got touched and that's a fucking no, no," LR spoke with ice in his voice. "There's no way the Queen is supposed to be in harm's way," LR continued, looking at all the runner's workers and generals. As he was talking, Ant and Uno walked into the room dressed in all black.

Walking to the front of the room, Uno winked at Punkin who stood in the front looking good in a Stella McCartney pants suit with some heels. Stepping back to stand next to Punkin, LR let Uno take over the room.

"I don't want to take over this meeting but shit is about to change right now as I speak. I have $5,000 for any of Red's people and if anyone of y'all brings me *Red* or info on him I have $50,000. To make it sweet for y'all, I have $20,000 for anyone of his generals," Uno said.

Everybody looked at one another because they never had that much money before. "I have said all I had to say to y'all. Tezzy, Lil E, and Fat D come holler at me over here," Uno said walking towards Ant.

"Tezzy and Fat D, this is my brother Ant. Lil E, you already know him," Uno said.

"What's up OG?" Fat D asked, looking at the man he'd heard so many ghetto stories about and had come to respect out of them. *I was thinking, from all the stories I have been hearing about Ant, he was big and mean. Really, he looks a little like Uno and they both have dreads*, Fat D thought to himself.

"Ant just gave him a head nod before turning to Tezzy and doing the same.

"Listen y'all, remember, when we were at the club, I told y'all needed something done," Uno asked looking at them.

"Yea," they all said at the same time."

"Well, I got some info on one of Red's right hands, so I need y'all to get at him ASAP. Here's a picture of his bitch and an address to one of the stores she owns. Her dude's name is Ride, he got that name because he is always down to ride and good with his gun, so don't make any mistakes," Uno said.

"We are on it," Lil E said. I also got some info from this bitch too Tezzy said.

"Ok, coo, y'all handle this and we will get on that other thing later, but if you have the info on you now, hand it to me, Uno said.

"I'm glad you made your mind up to fuck with me," Jimmy said to Red as he gave him a dap like they were old buddies.

"Yeah, it's simple. I will make more money fucking with you than with the plug I have now," Red said taking a seat in the chair across from Jimmy.

"I hope you're ready," Jimmy said, looking at Red.

"Ready for what?" Red asked, looking around.

"Ready to get this money," Jimmy said taking a sip of his drink.

"Listen Jimmy, I have been getting money since the 80s, so getting money isn't new to me. Feel me? Red said feeling a little disrespected.

"Well, I'm going to start you off with 350 bricks and see how they move first, then we will go from there. Is that coo? Jimmy asked, handing him two duffle bags.

Man-Man and Red sat in one of the stage spots breaking down the 350 bricks he just got from Jimmy.

"Boss….I'm high as hell in here off this shit. We have to get someone else to do this shit," Man-Man said rubbing his nose.

" Man, stop crying, we don't need anyone to know what we are getting, feel me?" We are about to get this money for real, without Uno having to plug the streets wide open." But on another note, I like how you handle the workers and the runners and the loyalty that runs through Yo's veins. But on the real, you really need to step your gunplay up, because you being in the position you are in, as my under Boss, you supposed to be head first in this war. You see me out here handling my business, making connects and shits so we can eat. Now it's time for you to do yours. I got us ready, set now, we are waiting on you so we can go cause we got a good thing going and we can't let Uno fuck it up," Red vented. "No, let's finish packing up this work so we can flood da streets.

Chapter 14

Tezzy, Lil E and Fat-D sat in Tezzy's all-black Infiniti truck across the street from the address Ant and Uno gave them.

"Look, we are just goin' to follow her and see where she takes us 'cause she might lead us right to the nigga Ride," Lil E said.

"Why don't we just grab the bitch now and make her tell us where he is at?" Fat D asked sitting up from the back."

"It's better my way," Lil E said, 'cause what if she doesn't talk? Then what?"

Ten minutes later, they saw the female locking up her store while she walked to her car. Tezzy started his engine.

"Damn, she is wearing them pants. Look at that ass!" Fat D said licking his lips. "The nigga Ride is doing real good for himself if his bitch own her own store," Fat D said more to himself.

They followed the female for about twenty minutes until she pulled her car in front of a nice-looking two-story house out in Greenwood, Indiana.

Shawn pulled up in front of her house and killed the engine. The only thing on her mind is shower, cooking for Ride and getting some sleep.

Opening her store from 8 a.m. until 10 p.m. at night, Shawn stayed on her feet and today she never had the time to rest.

Grabbing her bag off the floor on the passenger side of the car, she never saw Tezzy pull his truck up a few houses down from hers.

The trip thought they were tripping when they didn't see the chick anymore.

"Damn, did da bitch get out Tezzy thought to himself as he squinted and strained his eyes. Just as he was about to open his mouth the woman's head appeared rite before the driver's door opened.

Lil E and Fat D hopped out of the truck and ran to open the driver's door.

"Bitch, get up out of this car!" Lil E yelled as he grabbed her by their hair."

"Let me go! Please let me go!" Shawn screamed and kicked at her assailant.

"Dumb ass bitch stop yelling before I kill your ass out here," Lil E warned, shoving 9 mm into her scalp.

Tezzy jumped out of the truck and grabbed Shawn's keys and walked up to the house to let himself in.

I'm going to get straight to the point. Where is Ride, and where is all the dope?" Tezzy asked, slapping her dead in her mouth.

"What dope are you talking about?" Shawn asked.

"Bitch, you must think this shit is a game. You tell us, or I will just kill you now, Tezzy said, grabbing a knife off the counter." Now I'm going to ask one more time. Where is the dope and Ride?"

"I don't know what you're talking about." Shawn cried. Tezzy smiled as he grabbed her by the hair and cut off one of her ears.

"I don't know anything, Shawn managed to say between crying and screams."

"I see you want to keep playing," Tezzy said grabbing her again

"Please, please stop. I don't know anything."

"Man, that's enough," Lil E said, stepping in. "If she knew something, she would have told us by now."

Tezzy looked at Shawn and hit her with a three-piece knocking her out cold.

"Why the fuck you knock the bitch out? You are a silly ass nigga. Slow the fuck down sometimes nigga." Lil E chided.

"We just going to chill and wait on the nigga to get here" Fat D chimed walking into the kitchen to grab something to snack on.

"Yeah good idea, Tezzy said, breaking down some good lime green loud. Lil E just shook his head.

It took Shawn ten minutes to finally start coming back around. Opening her eyes, she looked around trying to understand what was going on.

"What's going on?" She asked, sounding like she'd been drinking. Tezzy hopped up and grabbed her by the hair." God must be with you today because I'm going to ask you where the dope and money are one more time.

"Please! I swear I don't know anything that Ride does out there in the streets. I told him I never wanted to know," she said, starting to cry again.

"Listen Big bro, I don't think she knew anything, so fall back off the lady' Lil E said in Tezzy's ear."

"You right bro, my bad," Tezzy agreed, putting two shots in Shawn's head.

"Man, what the fuck?" Lil E asked shitty, "What are you doing?"

"Man, it's war. Fuck that bitch. If the shoe was on the other foot, they would kill one of ours. Aw, I forgot, you don't even tell us about your bitch. She is always out of harm's way," Tezzy said.

Lil E was about to say something before they heard someone putting the key in the door. The three of them watched the door swing open, and Ride walked in.

"Bab—" his words trailed off as a look of go with a hint of fear stained his face. Always one to believe it is better to go out standing on his ten toes than on his two knees, Ride tried to up his pole.

Bak! Bak! Before Lil E guns finished smoking, Tezzy was already dragging Ride into the house and disarmed him. "Fat D lock the door," Tezzy yelled as he took a .45 out of the small of Ride's back and .380 off his waist.

"What the fuck y'all niggas want? Ride asked, clutching his bleeding legs.

"We want everything you have nigga" Lil E said, with a no-nonsense voice.

"I got 20 bricks and about $300,000 dollars, Ride said.

"Where is it nigga? Tezzy asked.

"I have another crib."

"Where at nigga?" Lil E asked.

"Around the corner," Ride said, "on Sunny Dr. 18130."

"Go grab that shit y'all" Lil E said, grabbing a chair. He began tying Ride to it." Now if that shit is not there, you will meet Shawn" Lil E said, nodding towards her body.

"Man, why y'all kill my baby, Ride asked, letting a few tears roll down his face.

About five minutes after Tezzy and Fat D left, Lil E looked at Ride sitting in the chair.

"Let me ask you something," Lil E said. "If you could trade your life for Red's would you?" Lil E wanted to know.

"Fuck you. You better kill me, 'cause if you don't I promise I'ma kill your whole blood line." Ride said.

In another life, I could see us as friends, Solid man," Lil E said, hearing his phone ring. He spoke for a few minutes before getting up and shooting Ride in the head twice.

Chapter 15

Uno pulled up in front of Talya and Skylar's restaurant he and Ant owned. He stepped out of his money-green Range Rover and immediately got a funny feeling in his gut.

"Yo, you need to hurry up," Uno said to Punkin as he made sure he had his pistol and two knives he always kept on him just in case.

Even since the takeover started, it hadn't gone through as planned. Uno had been paranoid, especially since Punkin almost got touched. Punkin almost getting touched should have never happened and Uno realized if anything ever happens to her, it would crush him and their daughter. Uno always thought about the situation he put Punkin in by letting her be in the street but if the situation was a test, she would have aced it with flying colors. With LR and her having the same bloodline and modeling skills as Uno, he knew if she was put against the ropes, she would find a way out.

"Baby, are you ok?" Punkin questioned, seeing the look Uno had on his face.

"I'm good baby," Uno said walking behind her, looking around. Punkin felt in her bones that something was wrong with Uno but she left it alone and walked into the restaurant.

"Hello, I have a table for two under the last name Brandon," Uno said, looking around at his investment. After the waitress made sure they were on the list, she escorted them to a table in the back. "Here you are," the waitress said trying to hand them their menus.

"We are good," Uno said. "Just give my lady the sauteed chicken breast, wild white rice and a caesar salad. I will have the classic twice-cooked pork on a bed of yellow rice with the best wine you have Uno said sitting back.

"A great choice, I'll be back with your meals shortly," the waitress stated before walking off.

"So how have you been?" Uno asked Punkin. He was looking her directly in her eyes the way he knew she loved. It was a look reserved only for her; a look of intense love and almost primitive lust that always made her feel like she was the only woman on earth for Uno.

"I've been okay, I guess since I'm around you more now," Punkin replied, returning her man's gaze. Since the attempt on her, Uno had been keeping her by his side daily and Punkin was enjoying every second of it. The love birds sat confabulated and laughing until the waitress returned with an expensive bottle of red wine.

"Your meal will be ready in a few minutes" the waitress informed them.

"Isn't this nice?" Punkin asked while allowing the fresh citrusy flavor of the elegant wine to decorate her palate.

"Yeah, it is," Uno nodded in agreement. His stomach growled and he was glad to see the waitress heading in his direction with plates in hand.

"Okay, you all enjoy your meal," the waitress encouraged, after laying out both of their dishes and unveiling the theme. "And if there's anything I can get for you, just holler," the waitress finished with a smile.

"Thank you," Punkin said to the waitress before she whisked off towards the kitchen.

As the pair talked and enjoyed their meal, Uno never saw the round, light-skinned man who favored Fat Joe from Terror Squad enter the restaurant.

"Uno what's happening?" Duffle Bag greeted him, walking past Uno's table towards him. "I need to get with you," Duffle Bag said over his shoulder.

"Baby, who was that?" Punkin asked, looking at the well-dressed man and lady.

"One of Omar's old grinding buddies. About twenty minutes later, Uno asked the waitress for the check and when she returned to the table with the receipt, she had a note from Duffle Bag. A number with ASAP written on it. Giving the waitress his card to return to Duffle Bag, he and Punkin left the restaurant.

Escorting Punkin out of the restaurant, Uno looked around b-cuz the eerie feeling was back again. Uno was not hearing anything Punkin was talking about as he zoned out his antennas in overdrive.

Meanwhile, across the parking lot, Man-Man sat in the passenger seat of a stolen Magnum while one of his flunkies Mac was in the driver seat.

"You sure they're inside that restaurant?" Man-Man asked, getting tired of sitting there and waiting on Uno to come out.

"Yea my female cousin just texted me and told me he was there. She even told me what they ordered. As he was talking, his phone began to ring loud. Picking up the phone and only speaking for a few minutes, he looked at Man-Man and smiled. "She said they were walking out now," Mac said. "There they go right there," Mac said, pointing at Uno and Punkin who were walking through the parking lot.

Getting out of the car Man-Man grabbed his .40 cal off his waist. "Listen you need to pull up down the block and wait just in case they run. Feel me?" Man-Man said.

"Baby, I'm going to beat that pussy up," Uno said as he hugged Punkin from the back.

"I bet you tell all these little hoes that,,," Punkin said looking over her shoulder. Punkin saw a man walking fast towards them. With it being dark, she couldn't see that well. "Baby there is a man behind us," Punkin said spinning out the hold Uno had on her with her .380 aimed at the dude and let off three shots landing one in his chest.

Uno grabbed his .40 cal and let off a few of his own shots before pushing Punkin down to the ground,

POW! POW! BAK! BAK! FAH! FAH!

Ducking down low, Uno and Punkin ran through the parking lot like their lives depended on it. Uno could tell whoever was shooting really didn't want to get the job done. That's good for me he thought. Ironically, Uno could feel something other than his heart beating. Watching Punkin in action, handling her business like a true gangsta bitch had Uno's dick throbbing.

On the next block, their sprint turned into a jog before becoming just a power walk. As they neared the middle of the street, they saw another man standing there in all black holding a gun. Uno raised his .40 and sent two shots in the dude's direction, hitting him in the arm before he ducked behind a tree.

Mac came from behind the tree letting off shot after shot as he ran towards Uno. Uno counted the bullets. When he knew the dude's clip was empty, he came from behind the car frying his gun "run". Uno told Punkin.

"Bros, we have to come back on this nigga real hard, but we have to come together so we can do it right and end this shit," Uno said, speaking to LR, Nasty, Lil E, Fat D, and Tezzy.

"Has anyone seen Mo-Mo because I haven't seen him in a while?" LR asked looking around the table. So we need to send someone to check on him ASAP.

"Man, this dude Red almost touched y'all twice and the streets are talking like y'all washed up," Fat D said looking from Nasty to LR then Uno.

"Nigga, I don't move b-cuz of what the streets are talking about. I'm a boss, so I move like one." Uno said hotly.

"I still got that info you gave me Tezzy, are you trying to get on that tonight?" Uno asked.

With a twisted-up mug, Tezzy let the sound of his pistol cocking back answer Uno's question.

"Also here's your cut of that Ride thing Lil E said handing Uno a bag.

Chapter 16

Man-Man, Black, and Big Head sat in a dark-colored jeep a half block away from where Nasty stood giving orders to his soldiers. They had been following Nasty for the past few days trying to see if he had a routine he did every day.

"I'm about to get up outta here. Keep the block on lock so strap the fuck up," Nasty said before hopping in his gray F-150 and pulling off down the street. When Nasty pulled out into traffic, he noticed that the jeep did too.

Man-Man tried to blend in with traffic on the road, unaware that he'd already been made.

"These niggas gotta be some fucking rookies," Nasty said to himself laughing as he looked through his rearview. He grabbed his .45 off his waist and sat it on his lap as he pulled up in front a nice-looking white house on Kenwood.

Seconds later, Man-Man noticed Ashley, a female they used to go to school with slid into Nasty's truck,

"Hey baby," Ashley said as she gave Nasty a kiss on the cheek leaving lipstick on his face.

"What's going on?" I see you got all dolled up for a nigga," Nasty said, looking down at her legs, at the same time trying to focus on the jeep. "You trying to go eat?"

"Sounds good to me, why not?" Ashley answered looking at Nasty just as lustfully.

Coming to a stop light, Nasty tried to look for the jeep but his eyes ended up landing at a motel across the street. A look of surprise was written on Nasty face.

"Baby, are you ok?" Ashley asked.

"Yea, I'm good baby," Nasty said pulling off and making a note to self to remind the family he saw Mo-Mo looking bad coming out of a motel.

Nasty pulled up to a fancy-looking restaurant a few blocks down the road. Before stepping out of the F-150, Nasty made sure his .45 was cocked. This shit is crazy, I'm getting too old for this shit, Nasty thought to himself as he parked.

When Mo-Mo saw that they were stopping at the restaurant, he told Black to take the wheel while he and Big-Head jumped out, walking fast but normal, trying not to be seen. They headed in Nasty's direction with a look like a lion on a hunt.

As Nasty told Ashley how good she smelled, he slowly grabbed his .45 off his waist and held it tight in his hand never breaking stride while surveying the parking lot for the jeep that had been following him. Looking behind him, he saw two men walking towards him with murder in their eyes.

"Listen babe, I need you to start running and don't look back or stop until you're inside the restaurant," Nasty instructed Ashley in a low voice. "Go," he said, spinning around and letting off a few shots so he could also have enough time to run. Inside the restaurant, Nasty let his rocket blast off three more missiles, over his shoulder.

Man-Man and Big Head got low dodging shots as they followed Nasty inside the restaurant. When all the people heard the gunshots, they hit the floor.

When Big Head looked up, he saw Nasty walking quickly towards the kitchen. Without hesitation, Big Head aimed and sent two shots in Nasty directions which only made the screaming customers get louder.

Nasty hit the kitchen door and noticed a waitress drop a tray full of plates before hitting the floor herself. As she lay on the bed of food, Nasty watched the two red stains on her chest grow bigger and darker and just shook his head. His heart went out to the waitress' family. Hopping up, Nasty made it to the back door and found out it had a chain and lock on it. He quickly sent two shots at the chain. The bullets hit the lock and chain causing it to snap.

When Nasty heard the gunman come into the kitchen, he kicked the door with all his might causing it to fly open.

"Fuck! We missed again" Man-Man yelled, knowing they were going to come back hard on them. Making it outside, Man-Man and Big Head ran around the corner to the waiting jeep.

A few hours later, Nasty stood in the room with LR, Uno and Ant snapping.

"It's on and popping now got dammit. They tried to get me, and Punkin out of here and they touched y'all two," Nasty said pointing at Uno and LR.

"This nigga Red must be fucking crazy" LR laughed loudly before he continued. Sending rookies at us like we are not true head ringers.

"We know better than him for not already having ended this shit a long time ago," Uno said, "but they've fucked with the right family."

We gotta handle these ourselves I see, b-cuz trying to play around is going to get everybody around us killed," Ant said taking a sip of his beer.

"I have seen that nigga Mo-Mo too walking into the motel down from the restaurant. He was looking like he was on that shit, so we should get somebody on him on the real bro. The nigga haven't been heard first in this war with us for a few weeks "Feel me?" Nasty said.

Taking his phone out, Uno dialed Tezzy's number.

"Hello, Tezzy listen, I need you to go to Motel Jump in Speedway and see if you can find Mo-Mo. Don't do anything just watch him 'cause he hasn't been the same, feel me?" Uno said, ending the call.

Chapter 17

Red paced around the room until he stopped at the bar. "We can't keep missing," he said looking at Man-Man, Black, Big Head, and Two-Tall, "cause they really not missing when they come, and as y'all know, we didn't have a lot of shooters from the start.

"I guess we're going to have to find us some new shooters then," Man-Man said puffing on his blunt.

It shouldn't be hard to find some niggas willing to get their hands dirty for a little money," Black assures his partners.

"Nah, I'm not fucking with just anyone. These niggas are pros. We have already been sleeping on Uno and 'em, so I'm trying to start off fresh this time, you dig? I'm recruiting all the new shooters myself and I know where I'm going to get them," Red said.

"Where? Because everybody knows you are at war with Uno," Two-Tall asked.

"I'm going to call my people in New Jersey," Red said. The vibration of Red's phone started again. He checked the caller ID to see who was being so persistent. The number belonged to Tiffany and Red answered this time, "What's up baby?" He asked.

"I see you a lovely dovely ass nigga," Uno laughed into the phone.

"Who is this? And why the fuck are you over my lady's house? Red asked while his mind started racing. He just moved Tiffany into a condo out in Fisher, so hearing a man's voice on her house phone caused Red to raise an eyebrow. Dots began connecting and it was then that he found out that Uno wasn't pulling any punches anymore and that he wanted to play hardball with the big boys. Red had little love for Tiffany, so he didn't want to see anything happen to her. Writing down Tiffany's address, he handed it to Man-Man. Covering the phone with his hand, get to that address now, all y'all! Red ordered.

The voice on the other end spoke again, "You know who this is, nigga? You know I really don't get my hands dirty anymore unless I have to. Instead, I hire goon squads to take care of everything, but I will tell you this; I'm going to give you what you are scared to ask for.

Shutting his eyes, Red pictures Tiffany's smile for the last time cause he knew she was gone and about to swim with the fishes.

"Uno continued to talk to Red" I know you get my message, now either fallback or I will have you and everybody you love killed."

"Uno, I hope you don't think you're going to win this. See, I'm from the old school, Red said. The old school of New Jersey and we whack shit for fucking fun, so let's get it on mu'fucka."

"It's about to get deep now," Uno said, hanging up.

As Nasty, Punkin and Ant packed boxes with pure cocaine inside Omar's Cuts owned by Ant, Uno and Nasty, they watched the news on the 72" smart TV.

"We are here today at Golden Park in Fishers on the city Northside, where a woman was murdered. The lady was found with the word "War" carved into her chest. The IMPD doesn't have any suspects in custody now and is asking that anyone who has any information come forth so that Justice can be served. And a grieving family can have closure. Now we have had 20 shootings and 10 murders in the last week. Law enforcement and ten-point coalition imploring the community to step up to help keep the streets safe. If you see or hear anything, call the number at the bottom of the screen.

"We will have more for you tonight at 10 pm. Reporting live from the city's Northside, this is Brittany Jones.

After they finished packing the boxes, a worker came and took them out to a waiting Fat-D. When Nasty and Punkin hopped in their car a police officer came zooming down the street and stopped in front of the car blocking them in. Punkin sat there calm but shitty.

"What can I do for you officers?" Punkin asked, smiling while the police walked up to them.

"You can wipe that pretty smile off your face" the fat cop spat, looking inside the car.

"I have a license and registration sir," Nasty said handing them to Punkin so she could give them to him. While the police walked off to check Nasty's info out, Ant stepped outside to see why everybody was standing around and when he saw what the police officer was doing, he walked over to him and spoke a few words in his ear. Handing Nasty's license back, the cops jumped back in the car and pulled off. Ant walked up to Nasty "My Bad" he said, handing him his stuff back.

Tezzy watched as Mo-Mo kept coming and going out of the motel room for days. He had to admit that Mo-Mo kept coming and going out of the motel room for days. He had to admit that Mo-Mo was carrying panties in a storage bag but he hadn't seen any female come out in the last few days he'd been watching him. Tezzy watched Mo-Mo come out and hop in his Lexus and drive off.

Walking to the front office, Tezzy entered and saw a pretty Spanish female behind the counter.

"Hello? How are you doing?" Tezzy asked, walking up to her. "Can I rap to you for a minute please?" He requested looking her in the eyes. "See my brother is in room 600 and I'm trying to get the key 'cause he's on the other side of town and I'm not trying to wait on him," Tezzy explained lying four fifty's on the counter.

"Shid, you can keep the money if you promise to take me out," she said looking him up and down. Grabbing his phone off his belt, he typed in her number." What's your name?" He asked her.

"London and yours," she shots back.

"Everybody calls me Tezzy."

"Well, I get off work at 9:30 pm if you are trying to meet up," London said, handing him their key card.

"Where do you stay? 'Cause I might just slide down on you later," Tezzy said.

"I stay in the apartment on the corner of 38th and BLVD apt 18," she told him.

"Ok, I'll be at you," Tezzy said, walking out of the office,

Mix Breed opened her eyes, blinking away the fog as she tried to remember where she was at. All she knew was that she had been in this motel for a long time and that Mo-Mo wasn't planning on letting her go. He kept her high and chained up 24/7. She was his own personal sex slave. Trying to get the image out of her mind, she started to cry. Her life had been in a downward spiral since... Since that night at the party when she hit da primo. She shook her head at what wanting to fit in had gotten her into. Hard fucking time.

She thought about every person that had done her wrong while she traveled on the long hard road of addiction. Even she was on the list because she knew she was the one feeding herself the poison, but Mo-Mo and Punkin still held the top spots on her list.

It was at that moment that Mix Breed, filled with hope, made a promise to herself to get clean. And she'd never been more sincere than she was now. That in part came from the second part of her promise to herself.

A fire had been lit under her ass and her sights were set on eyes and teeth but Mix Breed understood that in order to get revenge on all those on her shit list, she'd have to be strong and sober.

The door opening and shutting drew Mix Breed from her thoughts. Faking sleep, Mix Breed peeked to see what Mo-M was doing. Seeing the dude walk into the light, she realized it actually wasn't Mo-Mo.

"Please! Please! Help me!" Mix Breed screamed. Tezzy's face twisted when he saw that Mix Breed was chained to the heater on the wall like she was a dog. Quickly unchaining her got to his car and drove off disgusted as he tried to figure out Mo-Mo's rationale.

Dialing a number, Tezzy waited. "Uno man, Mo-Mo needs to be dealt with like ASAP. He had Mix Breed chained up to a fucking heater in the motel like a pet," Tezzy said.

"Hello, Mix Breed said into the phone with a cracking voice.

"Amber, I'm sorry. I'm going to have Tezzy drop you off at one of my cribs on Kenwood. You can stay there as long as you want and everything you will need is there, even some money," Uno said before hanging up.

Chapter 18

Fred had just gotten off the phone with some of his sources in Indianapolis and didn't know whether to be glad or disturbed about what he just heard.

The word was that the Mexicans are behind Red. They are mad that Uno stopped fucking with them on the dope and they felt that Uno had robbed them. So, hooking up with Red was a win-win for the Mexicans. They felt they could get Uno out of the way while still having a hold on the streets through Red.

Now that Fred knew of the wet back's plan, he had to help Uno. He and Uno were making a lot of money together, plus Uno was his connect to Indianapolis so it was only right.

Being a punctual nigga, Ant pulled his all-black Cadillac Escalade sitting on 26' in front of Club Sexy Lady. It was 10:29 pm, a minute before the time Fred had asked him to be there.

When he walked up to the door, the guard already knew who he was.

"Follow me sir," the guard instructed, walking to an office in the back of the club. "Drink," the guard offered.

"Naw, I'm good. Thanks. All I want is for you to go grab your boss so I can get out of here."A few minutes later, a clean-shaved guy came into the office.

"What's good?" My name is Pook" he said walking up to Ant.

"What's good my dude? Why am I here?" Ant asked getting right to the point of the meeting.

"Well, Fred sent you a little something, something that's important. Follow me and I will show it to you my nigga," Pooh said. They walked down a hallway before entering a dimly lit room. When Ant walked in, he laid eyes on what had to be the biggest Artillery he had ever seen in his life.

"What the fuck is going on?" Ant said, opening a box.

"See, after your brother started messing with Fred, Jimmy was shitty, so he hooked up with Red and his crew and started hitting them off with dope. Well, let's just say the shit Jimmy pulled didn't sit well with Fred, and so this is his way of showing it.

"I will have someone come to grab these guns in the next few days, Ant said adjourning their meeting.

Mix Breed walked into the IMPD Precinct out west and with mixed emotions, she knew it was a better way to go about getting her retribution. A way that didn't have the potential to hurt those who had compassion for her. But vindictiveness was mu'fucka and it got the best of her.

"I need to speak with someone," she screamed. "Someone important 'cause I hear there is a reward out for any information on all the murders going on in the streets."

The bustling office had quieted and the floor was all Mix Breed's. Anybody with eyes could see that Mix Breed was rationally emotional. And every veteran officer knew the value of a scorned woman.

Lt. John Spell stepped out of his office looking for the cause of all the commotion. It didn't take long for him to spot the black woman at the front desk who was still screaming out murder talk.

"Hello, my name is LT. Spell," he said, offering his hand. She shook it. "And mine is Amber" she said in response looking the handsome LT up and down.

Spell was light-skinned brother with bride shoulders and a ill baby 'fro. He had a clean face and looked to be in his late twenties or early thirties. Mix Breed's stare down did nothing for Spell because off the top, he knew she was on drugs.

"What can I do for you miss?" Spell asked.

"Really sir, it's not about what you can do for me, but what I can do to help you out."

"I'm listening" Spell stated, not jumping to any conclusion. Over the years, he'd heard this same song sang time and time again.

"Well, there are a lot of murders happening in the streets and I'm sure I can help you clean. 'Em up sir. Plus I hear there's even a reward out for any information leading to an arrest."

So this is what this is about, Spell thought. Mix Breed could tell the LT was about to dismiss her so she thought quickly. She couldn't lose the chance of getting back and coming up at the same time.

"One of the men responsible for the killing kidnapped me. I escaped...Well, I was rescued the other day by another man who's affiliated with WSF." Mix Breed blurted out and immediately regretted it. In no way did she intentionally want to implicate Tezzy, but her desperation got the best of her.

The realization of her slip-up was all over her face and Spell picked up on it. "Come this way Amber," LT instructed walking towards his office.

He took a seat across from the young lady and noticed a look of uncertainty on her face. He knew only two reasons that produced that look, which were cold feet and guilt. He didn't think a junky was capable of guilt, so he assumed it had to do with the reward money.

In reality, tho the money was already hers, she'd had him at kidnapped and WSF, but he'd never let her know that.

"Okay, now what can you tell me? And if the information checks out, you will be compensated," LT. Spell assured her.

"Well, I know all about the war going on in the streets and who's behind it." Mix Breed spent an hour and a half writing down names, locations and dates she could remember, but she never gave up on Nasty, Uno or Tezzy directly.

Mo-Mo walked into his motel two days later with bags in his hand. He'd been shopping for himself and Mix Breed and couldn't wait to smoke some dope and fuck the shit outta his new sex toy.

For the past few weeks, he'd been holding her hostage up in the motel with no intent of letting her go. He knew Uno and 'em was probably looking for him but he didn't want them to see him fucked up.

Mo-Mo walked to the heater and saw Mix Breed's chain lying on the floor and panicked. Grabbing all his stuff, he ran out of the room and hopped back into his car. Dialing Nasty number, Mo-Mo waited for him to pick up.

"Bra? This Mo-Mo where y'all at? I need to pull up on y'all real fast.

"We at the spot on 10th in Dearborn you will see us," Nasty said.

Chapter 19

"This shit done got personal," Red said taking on a blunt. He killed my bitch man," he added hitting the table.

"So what are you going to do about it?" Jimmy asked, looking at Red.

"Somebody gon' have to die, cause I'm tired of playing with this little bitch ass dude. I been giving him a pass because of his brothers but that's over with," Red said sternly.

"Fuck it; I got some people ready to roll rite mufukin now. All I have to do is make the call," Jimmy said, grabbing his phone off the desk.

"Nah, I'm good I have my own people coming in soon. This shit is not going to end until one of us is dead."

"I have a plan," Jimmy said standing now. I heard every year they get together and throw a party for whomever soul day is coming up, and guess who's soul day is up next? Jimmy asked with a smile,

"Who? Jimmy stop playing with me," Red said.

"LR's" Jimmy stated.

"All we have to do is grab one of their people to see where the party is and we have them," Red said.

"Listen man, I have a female friend that told me she saw Punkin coming and going from this address," Jimmy said handing Red a piece of paper. "I don't know if the address is 100% tho," he admitted.

Uno pulled up in Duffle Bag's long Cobblestone Driveway thinking, Dayum, this mu'fucka is nice. Parking behind a baby blue BMW, Uno hopped out and just stood for a few moments taking in the house curve appeal. The home was like a palace, one fit for a King.

"So, this is what a nigga does when he retires Uno thought out loud.

Duffle Bag had been a heavyweight in the game back when Uno was knee-high to a grasshopper. Selling major weight and more pills than a pharmacy is how Duffle Bag got his name and his success.

And until one traumatic night, he'd been sitting back enjoying a long and prosperous ride. But like the saying goes, all good things come to an end. And on that hospital bed, body riddled with bullet holes, that's exactly what Duffle Bag thought; it was the end.

So when he walked out— no, even *before* he walked out of that ER room, he'd made the smart choice to fall the fuck back from the streets for good.

After ringing the doorbell, Uno waited patiently for a response.

"Hello, how you doing sir?" The man asked opening the door before stepping to the side to allow Uno entry. Following the man through the mansion, Uno looked around amazed a little. Even tho he had money, he never thought about buying a mansion like this. Uno stepped into Duffle Bag's office and saw the beautiful woman that had accompanied Duffle Bag the night they saw each other at the restaurant, sitting at the table beside Duffle Bag.

The woman wore a black Coogi pants suit with the pumps that matched. Her hair was pulled up in a bun that sat on top of her head, and she had bangs that stopped right above her eyes; the style gave her a foreign look.

"Uno, have a seat," Duffle Bag said as he poured three drinks. He handed one to the lady and slid the other one over to Uno.

"Breezy, this is Uno, Uno this is Breezy, my niece. Breezy's here to handle some business for me. I was glad I bumped into you at dinner that night because I've been trying to get at you for the longest. We can help each other," Duffle bag said looking at Uno.' I know you're at war with Red and I can hand you his head on a silver platter, but you have to help Breezy with some important shit for me."

"And what's that?" Uno asked, sipping his Louis XIII cool, calm and composed.

"Rest in peace my niggah," Duffle Bag thought as the poker face Uno was wearing reminded him of Omar. "I need you to help her with the enforcement. Yes I know you are your own boss, but you run these streets, so you can show her around."

"Ok, that's cool with me. What about you?" Uno looked at Breezy. "I'm cool too," she said licking her lips.

"Good" Duffle Bag said handing Uno, Red's info, Uno took it but didn't know if should've been shitty at how Duffle Bag seemed to already know the outcome of this meeting or impressed.

"I need y'all to handle this here ASAP if you are not busy Uno." Duffle Bag said. "Also, you know I've been pushing that loud now, the dope game is over for me ever since I got shot up and plus I'm getting too old," Duffle Bag said laughing. "Aye Breezy, let me holler at Uno solo bolo rite quick," he stated.

"Okay Unc," Breezy said, getting up to make her exit. Duffle Bag watched the inevitable take place, as Uno watched Breezy stab off like a model. He couldn't help but smirk because he knew with an ass like Breezy's a man could not stare.

Just as Breezy disappeared, Duffle Bag cleared his voice. "Uh Un" Uno slowly returned his gaze back to Duffle Bag whose smirk had been replaced with seriousness.

"That's my niece niggah, so keep her safe." Duffle Bag said.

Breezy burned rubber through the city like Danicka Patrick, listening to Uno's instructions on where to go. Even though she kept her eyes on the road, she could sense Uno's gaze on her and it was making her hot. Although it was a rare occurrence, Breezy was attracted to Uno almost immediately.

From his long beautiful locs and boss nigga demeanor to the perfect smile she hadn't seen him wear since that night at the restaurant when he was with an ole girl.

"Bitch stayed focused, he's off limits, and she coaxed herself. Pull up right here," Uno said, pointing to the side of the club. "When we get in there, we gon' handle our business and get out of there. Feel me?"

Inside the club, four dudes were sitting around drinking and talking. "Hey, we're closed, y'all have to get out," one of the dudes barked.

"Muthafucka, does it look like we care if y'all closed?" Uno said, sending a bullet through the dude's head. Turning towards the other two men, Uno let his .45 bark sending bullets two by two into one of their bodies, while Breezy sent a bullet through the remaining one's eye.

"Go grab what your uncle is looking for," Uno commanded walking back to the front of the club, while Breezy scrambled around looking for whatever her uncle asked of her. Uno double-checked and made sure that the four dudes had officially left the planet.

"Got it!" Breezy said as she returned from upstairs holding at Uno with even more respect.

Chapter 20

"It's about time you got here," London said stepping to the side so Tezzy could enter her apartment.

"My bad baby, I had to go pick up some smoke before I came through," Tezzy said, already high off the blunt he smoked. Tezzy had to do a double take when he noticed London wearing some pink booty shorts with some heels on alone with a little t-shirt. Baby's body was stupid dumb silly and he couldn't wait to peel her clothes off and fuck the shit out of her.

"I thought you weren't coming over for a minute," London said looking at Teezy. So, how was your day?" she asked.

"It was coo" he stated sitting back on the sofa.

"So do you have family around here?" she asked.

"Nah, not around here. My people stay out east. I have a mom, a few sisters and brothers. My father is around but we won't be fucking around with each other like that."

Pouring herself a drink, London down it all at once! The Grey Goose instantly had an effect on her. Her mind went back to when Tezzy walked into her job with his fine ass. Her body starts heating up.

"Fuck it Shid, I'm about to get that dick," London said to herself, "I need to ask you another question," London said moving over towards Tezzy and putting her legs in his lap.

"Go head," Tezzy said as his dick got hard from looking at her fat ass pussy print.

"Do you have a girlfriend? And what exactly are you looking for because I don't have time for games. I'm grown and you are too, so if you got a girl just getting dick from you but if you get this pussy, it would be yours and yours only. Feel me sexy?" London said with a smile.

Leaning back further on the sofa, Tezzy just looked at her, pleased by the game she'd just kicked at him.

"Listen, I don't have a girl at home but do have two baby mommas and a lot of female friends that I do fuck with, but that doesn't mean anything, you feel me? cause like you said, we are both grown," Tezzy said lighting a blunt. "If I find out you giving that pussy to another nigga, it's over for the both of y'all. I'm a boss man, so you need to hold yourself like a boss lady.

Leaning over, London grabbed Tezzy's face and planted a big wet kiss on his lips. Tezzy lifted London onto his lap while taking her shirt off, exposing her pretty round breast.

"I will be right back," London said as she stood up and stripped off her clothes, before heading to wherever she was going. London's ass was so fat, it just jiggled like crazy with every step she took.

"Hurry up and bring that ass over here to Bossman," Tezzy said as London walked over to him.

"Damn nigga, you are still dressed? You are not getting this pussy, drink or blunt until you ass hole naked." Without thinking twice, Tezzy got to donning his birthday suit. When Tezzy hit the sofa, London handed him his blunt and drink and grabbed the remote to turn the music up. London started shaking her ass as Tezzy chilled on the sofa. Playing with his dick, Tezzy stood up and walked up to London and grabbed her.

"Playing time is over with," he whispered in her ear while carrying her across da room. When he got her to the sofa, he sat her down and she opened her legs wide.

"Ssss" they both hissed in harmony as Tezzy's girth filled London's tight wet pussy.

"Easy Papi," London moaned as she wrapped her legs around Tezzy while pulling him in more. Tezzy then took London's legs and relocated them on top of his shoulders, as he stood up making himself go deeper and deeper. He looked down and watched his dick disappear into the pussy. Flipping London over making her bend over the sofa, Tezzy slid back in and started beating that pussy up while his nuts hit her clit.

As London threw the pussy back on Tezzy, he slapped her ass aggressively. Teezy tried to look away from London's ass juggling but with her moans, he picked up speed.

"Beat this pussy up Papi," London moaned, rubbing her own clit. Tezzy couldn't hold on any longer as he pulled out and nutted all over London's back and ass.

"I'm a beast," Tezzy said, standing up with his barrel chest rising and falling feverishly.

"Whatever nigga, you better be loyal because I am," London said getting up and walking off to the bathroom smiling.

Ever since the day Mix Breed spilled her gut to LT. Spell, he'd been having a hard-on for WSF and Red's crew. A block down from one of Uno's drug houses, LT. Spell watched everything through state-of-the-art binoculars, sipping on coffee. He watched the continuous flow of traffic moving between Roach to 26th. Cars were everywhere while dudes ran from car to car. LT Spell couldn't wait to lock up both of the crews for life.

They'd been running around the city selling drugs and dropping bodies all over the place like they had a license for it. Spell knew that his main priority would be keeping Amber safe because without her, their super lawyers would destroy his entire operation. The bastards would most likely walk away with a slap on the wrist and Spell wasn't having that.

Dropping his binoculars, he looked down at the pictures of people Amber had given him and matched the faces of Punkin, Mo-Mo, and Fat-D to the ones on the block. Pulling off, Spell scowled as he rode past all the clogged traffic. It took everything in him not to hop out and started slapping cuffs on the low-life sons of bitches.

"Pull over!"

"We got that good!"

"Gimme a 20!" he heard various people yelling while he made his way slowly down the street with his teeth.

"What are you trying to get?" One of the runners asked, slapping Spell's truck as he rode past him. Spell stopped in the middle of the street and shot the runner a look that could kill before riding off. The only reason he kept going is that he saw the big fish.

For the past two hours, Man-Man and Red sat in the dark-colored jeep directly in front of the address Jimmy gave them. The whole time they sat in the car, the only light they saw was from the TV that was on.

"OG, I don't think anyone is coming or going Man-Man," said looking down at his phone. As they hopped out of the car, they checked to make sure the guns were locked and loaded.

"I need her alive, Red said standing behind Man-Man as he watched him kick in the door. Soon as the door hit the floor, Man-Man was quick on his feet running in with his P89 in the air. Stepping inside the house, Man-Man saw a female trying to run towards the back but he let off three shots hitting her twice in the head, painting the wall with her brains.

"Fuck, didn't I just tell your silly ass I need the bitch alive," Red said waving his gun in the air. "Now we're back at step one and Uno going to be on his toes."

"Shid my bad, I didn't mean to kill her, my aim was just on point, feel me?" Man-Man said. You want Uno? Well, best believe he will be coming after he finds his Queen. Looking at Punkin one last time, Red knew the war was about to reach its peak cause LR and Uno were going to turn the city into a straight fucking war zone until they find out who killed their family.

"Let's get out of here Man-Man said getting an ill feeling in his stomach.

Shaking his head, Red looked around the room one last time and down at the dead female and let two more shots off into her body before walking out the house like nothing ever happened, leaving a blood bath to clean up.

Chapter 21

Mo-Mo sat with his head in his hands thinking about how it was going to be a long day. He'd fuk'd up and he knew it. When he pulled up on the block the other day and hopped out, all the looks he got from the WSF members were the first signs of what was to come. They were like grey clouds before the storm.

He pulled on his New Port to calm his nerves. He could hear LR barking orders outside and knew where he was heading. Taking a deep breath, Mo-Mo prepares himself for LR to walk in, his footsteps getting closer and closer.

"What the fuck been on nigga?" LR asked looking at Mo-Mo.

"Just stressing man, you know how it is," Mo-Mo said, looking everywhere but LR's eyes.

"Is our money correct on your part be-cuz I can't see how it would be when you've been on a whole lotta bullshit lately," LR said. Well, Uno wants to holler at you about that shit," LR told him before walking out of the room and Nasty followed by Tezzy came in to sit at the table.

Ten minutes passed before Mo-Mo looked up to see Uno walking in with a sexy female.

"Breezy, this is my family; Nasty, Tezzy and Mo-Mo. I don't know where my other brother is but this is Breezy."

"Hello," Breezy said in a sexy laid back voice. They all hit her back with a head nod. Walking to the bar to make himself and Breezy a drink, Uno came back and sat at the big round table. He let Mo-Mo sweat under his gaze before finally breaking the silence.

"I heard about the bullshit you were on in that motel."
"What the fuck were you thinking? Uno asked.

"Bro, I promise it's not what you think," Mo-Mo said, looking at a spot on the floor. Right then, Uno knew Mo-Mo couldn't be trusted anymore be-cuz he couldn't even look him in the eye.

"Fuck that crack-smoking ass whore, she owes me," Mo-Mo said.

"How does a crackhead owe you Mo-Mo?" Uno asked knowing he was about to lie.

"She owed the spot $100, so I was making her pay it off," Mo-Mo said. "Why do you care anyway? She ain't nothing but a crack whore anyway."

"Nigga, you need to be careful who you put down when you're on your high horse 'cause you're guaranteed to see some of those people you looked down on when you come tumbling back down on your ass, and from the looks of you, you already have started your tumbling cause you look like you have been smoking too," Uno said.

"Man, fuck you not all that," Mo-Mo said.

"What the hell are you just saying to me?" Uno asked looking at Mo-Mo.

"I didn't say anything, I didn't say anything bro."

LR walked into the room and was surprised Uno was there already. Sitting at the table with the guys, he saw a sexy female sitting back sipping her drink. Grabbing his ringing phone, LR picked up. After talking for a few minutes, LR got off and dropped to the floor.

"You good?" Uno asked rushing to LR" they got her man LR, said crying.

"Who got who?" Uno asked, unsure of what he was saying.

"They killed Punkin, shot her in the head," LR told them.

Enraged, Uno threw his glass at the wall breaking it on impact into a million pieces. Pulling his gun out, Uno sent three shots into Mo-Mo's body knocking him out of his chair.

"What's the hell Uno?" Nasty said jumping up from the table! "Why did you do that shit."

"Nigga, they just killed Punkin plus he is a broken link in our chair and he just paid for the sins of his sisters. Uno said sitting down. Would he have killed Mo-Mo under normal circumstances? Probably not but the only thing that could come from Uno seeing red was red.

"I don't know who this Punkin person is but I see she means something to you, so if there's anything I can do to help you, all you have to do is ask. You have shown me a good time since I have been around you," Breezy said in a low voice that made Uno look up at her.

"They're forcing me to do something they really don't wanna see," Uno said, slamming his fist on the table. Grabbing his phone, Uno dialed some numbers.

"Hello, what's up?" Big Bro, Uno said into the phone.

"What's good? Ant said immediately knowing something was wrong with Uno.

"I need you bro, they killed Punkin" Uno said.

"On my way," Ant replied, hanging up and heading to the airport.

Chapter 22

"Listen, I don't want no bullshitting when we get in there, no one gets to see tomorrow. Not even the pets," Uno said looking at Nasty, Ant, Tezzy, Lil E, LR and Breezy.

"I'm killing a few mu'fukas tonight," Tezzy said, rubbing his hands together.

"Me, Ant, and Breezy are going to take the car and y'all take the van," Uno said, watching them load their weapons.

"Yo, Man-Man you ain't ready to go yet, damn" Red yelled towards the back of the house.

"I'm on my way now," Man-Man yelled walking from the back "Boss do you think it's a good idea to go out right after what happened to Punkin?" Man-Man asked looking at him.

"We good nigga, come on. I'm ready to take my wife out to dinner for her birthday; with this war going on, I haven't really spent any time with her," Red said. Man-Man didn't protest any further for reasons of his own.

"The rest of you nigga's and bitches in here need to find something to do while we are gone, and y'all better have no more people over my house," Red said walking out of the front door.

As Man-Man drove off the block, he saw a car and van zooming down the block. Not paying them much attention, he continued pushing all of the 550 horse that the $224,600 Porsche Cayenne Turbo had down Guion Road. He had a need for speed and loved when Red pulled out the 4800 IB beast for special occasions.

"Me, Breezy and Ant are going through the front door, y'all take the back. Just in case somebody tries to run," Uno said.

When they reached the front door Uno kicked the door off the hinges. Breezy was the first one in the house followed closely by Ant.

"Everybody drop to the floor!" Breezy yelled, sending two shots into the dude standing closest to her. Who was moving too slow?"

Nasty, LR, and Tezzy came in from the back with two dudes at gunpoint, making them all lie on the ground in a line while Uno went down the line killing them execution style.

"We're going to wait until this bitch shows up," Uno said sitting down on one of Red's suede sofas.

Red and his wife were enjoying their meal while Man-Man sat close by, watching everything that moved.

"Thank you baby for spending my birthday with me, it means so much to me," Brittany said, sipping her Apple Martini.

"I'm sorry for not spending time with you lately, it's just that a lot has been going on, but as soon as it's over, I promise we goin' to take a trip," Red said.

"I'm ready to go so I can get myself some birthday sex," Brittany said licking her lips. "Check please," Brittany said as the waitress was walking past.

"Yo, Man-Man, you can drop yourself off and I will take the car from there," Red said, thinking about the good sex he was about to get tonight.

Twenty minutes later, Red pulled up in his driveway doing 60 before the Porsche stopped on a dime right in front of his 12-foot French doors. Brittany couldn't keep her hands off Red and tonight was a good night cause he has no problem getting a boner.

"Hold up, hold up baby. Give me five minutes before you come in," Brittany said, getting out of the car and walking into the house.

As soon as Brittany walked into the house, Tezzy grabbed her up and slapped the shit out of her.

"Bitch, why is he just sitting out there?" LR asked, slapping her in the mouth again.

"I told him to give me five minutes before he comes in" Brittany said crying. After the five minutes was up, Red walked into the house and got hit in the back of the head sending him down for the count.

"You grab this nigga and his bitch up and put them in the van," Uno instructed, while Ant and Breezy jumped into their car.

Chapter 23

LT. Spell had been at his desk for the past four hours going through the extensive case files he'd put together on the infamous bosses and their organizations. He moved each picture from row to row trying to see who was who and what their roles were.

As he put the pictures together, he could tell who were the runners, workers, watchers and lieutenants. While he sat at his desk, LT. Spell heard the dispatch asking for cars because a woman had been killed a few days ago by the name of Punkin Walton.

"That has to be the same Punkin," LT. Spell thought, grabbing his keys before running out of the office. There was no way he was going to let anyone stick their nose in his case and take his credit.

Fifteen minutes later, LT. Spell pulled up to the address he heard on dispatch. Jumping out, he walked into the house and saw a body under the white sheet.

"What do we have here?" Detective LT .Spell asked, pulling up the sheet.

"We have a female victim DOA two shots to the house and saw a body under the white sheet.

"What time of death are we looking at?" LT .Spell asked.

"Well around 2-3 in the morning, a few days ago.

When Red woke up he found himself in a basement, tied up to a chair.

"What the fuck is going on?" Red yelled, trying to get free of his hands. Looking around, Red saw what he believed to be the back of his wife, who was tied up to another chair with her head missing. Throwing up, Red started crying.

"No please, not my Brittany, Red yelled, hoping it wasn't her and even refused to believe it was. That was until he made out the three letters that made up his name through her bloody wrist. "Show your face like a man," Red said crying harder.

Uno and LR walked out from the dark right up to Red's chair with their shirts off. Uno bent down, so he was eye to eye with Red.

"You ready to talk to me?" Uno asked, dropping the chain he handed to the floor.

"Whatever you want," Red said looking from the chain to his wife, to the knife LR held with blood dripping from it.

"I want to know two things. Who had the balls to kill my woman 'cause by the looks of it, your crying ass couldn't be the one and the second one is, I want to know where I can find Jimmy," Uno said, picking the chain back up and hitting him again. When Red's screams subsided, he spoke.

"I'm sorry about Punkin Red," said looking at LR.

Slamming the knife he had in his hand down on Red knee, LR looked him in the eye.

"Nigga, don't speak of my sister's name, LR stated.

"I'm sorry but y'all were making me look weak in the streets, so Jimmy did some little digging and found out where Punkin was at, so he gave me the address and me and Man-Man went over there and killed her. I have five million if you let me go" Red said. Please. I didn't mean it," Red said scared to death.

Laughing, Uno dropped the chain at Red feet, sending a chilling feeling up his body." Now where is Jimmy?" Uno asked.

"I don't know where he stays but we always met at this house out east where we were ducked off."

Uno untied Red's left hand. "Write the address down and if you give me the five million you were talking about with Man-Man, I will let you walk out of here today with your life. The five million would go towards Punkin finally resting."

"Now that you have all the addresses, can I please go?" Red asked with some puppy dog eyes.

"Sorry" Uno said, picking up the chain and wrapping it around his neck while LR stabbed him all in the body.

"Uno and LR had been on a mission all day. Sitting in LR's car at the address that Red had given them, he began to grow impatient."

"Where the fuck is this weak ass nigga at?" LR said out loud.

"He will be here, be cool," Uno said.

Not even ten minutes later, Uno noticed a white Benz pull up in front of the address he had written down on the paper. Sitting up in the car, Uno wanted to see if Man-Man was going to hop out or not. Gripping his twin .45's, Uno looked over and saw LR doing the same.

Man-Man hopped out looking up and down the block. Walking to the other side of the car, he opened the door and started grabbing bags.

Once Uno and LR laid eyes on Man-Man, they hopped out of the car and walked quickly up the block. Sending two shots in Man-Man direction Uno hit the car window and the other shot hit Man-Man in the chest knocking him into the car door.

Dropping the bags, Man-Man grabbed his gun off the hip and got low. Man-Man's heart started beating a thousand miles a minute as he tried to think of a way out of this.

Come out and stop hiding bitch! LR yelled, slowly walking towards the car Man-Man was hiding behind.

"Damn, that's LR, so the other has to be Uno. Fuck, if I don't come up with a plan, they are going to kill me out here," Man-Man thought as he hopped up letting off four shots so he could get enough time to run.

Fuck! Uno yelled as he heard the police sirens getting louder. Moving fast back towards the car they hopped in and drove off mad at themselves.

Chapter 24

From all the limousines that lined the entrance, it looked like a big traffic jam. There was over twenty of them back to back.

Uno looked up to the sky and prayed to go to let God let Punkin through His gates as the sun through clouds.

"Thank you God," he said taking the sun poking out as a sign his prayers was being answered.

Punkin's had been placed on sand with white roses surrounding it. Uno and LR spent ten thousand just on the 14k gold casket alone. It seemed as if the whole city came out to show their respect to Uno and LR.

Uno gritted his teeth tightly as he thought about how he missed the opportunity to kill Man-Man so Punkin could rest in peace. There was something in the air, and everyone there knew the store was yet to begin.

As the preacher started talking, a black Lincoln Town car with tinted windows rolled up slowly and parked. There were so many cars out there that many people didn't pay it any mind but OG veteran's eyes knew what was up.

Hitting LR with his elbows, Uno nodded his head towards the car. LR looked back and knew exactly who it was; it was Jimmy. Rolling down the window Jimmy and Man-Man looked LR and Uno in the eyes while pulling off slowly.

After the service, Uno didn't have a destination. He just drove for hours while in dee thought. "I need to unwind some," Uno said to himself while putting up into Sunrise strip club's parking lot.

Hopping out the whip, Uno put his .357 on his hip. Knowing the bouncer, Uno entered the club unchecked. As soon as he stepped in, he saw women everywhere twerking, popping and doing acrobats. Uno made his way to a table in the corner so he could see the door. Sitting down, he waved the fine as the waitress passed. He ordered a bottle of Ace of Spades and asked for seven hundred dollar bills.

After the waitress sat his ones and bottle on the table, his eyes saw the most beautiful white stripper walking past. Waving money in the air, she looked at him and walked directly in front of him and started making her ass bounce and jiggle while she was standing still.

"Work for this money," Uno said throwing dollars at the stripper who was digging shit he had never seen. When the stripper saw that Uno was not healed, she started to really make her ass cheeks clap, making sounds and all. Sitting in his lap, she began to grind hard on Uno's dick. Uno just leaned back sipping from the bottle and watched her do her things.

"Yo no disrespect but is dancing all you do for money?" Uno asked.

"No disrespect taken, but yes, I'm doing this so I can pay my way through college," she whispered in his ear as she continued to move her body on Uno. She could tell he had something on his mind, something monstrous in between his legs.

"If you don't mind me asking, what's your name?" Uno asked.

"Everyone calls me Bunny," she said while looking him in the eyes and at herself.

"Everyone in the city calls me Uno," he said, looking back at her.

Bunny stopped moving when she heard his name. She has heard so much about him that just hearing his name made her pussy jump. She was glad she wasn't the type to just open her legs.

"I know that's not who I think it is," he said to himself as he gave the stripper a hand full of money as the song ended. Uno got up and headed over in the direction he was looking at.

"What the fuck you are doing in a strip club?" Uno asked walking up to the woman.

Breezy looked up with her nose in the air. Dudes had been trying to get at her since she had been in the club, so she thought it was another lame trying to fuck her until she looked up and saw Uno standing over her looking sexy.

"What's up Uno?" Breezy asked, smiling.

"I asked you what the fuck you are doing in here," Uno said sitting down next to her.

"Just need to get my mind off a lot of shit. Feel me?" Breezy said taking a sip of her drink." You know Duffle Bag needs some more shit handle plus I have my own thing going on."

"I know," Uno said taking a swig from his bottle. "I have a lot going on too but tomorrow is a new day. We can handle that shit for your Uncle, so that way you can have a little free time to see my city.

Breezy smirked. She knew with Uno's help, she would have her business done in no time. "So, what have you been up to?" She asked.

"You know I had to bury my daughter's mother today, but besides that, getting money."

After about two hours of talking, Breezy and Uno parted ways and promised to meet the next day.

Chapter 25

LR paced back and forth as he, Uno, Nasty, Tezz, Ant, Lil E, and Fat-D all held a conversation.

"Man, I'm telling y'all we have to find that nigga Jimmy before it's too late," LR said looking at everybody.

"Yea, I feel you Lil Bro, but we have to get our money all the way right cause Jimmy's money runs deeper than the Atlantic. We are not broke, by far, but at the same time when we gun for him, every dot has to connect." Uno said putting the TV on.

"What do you think we should do?" LR asked.

"Hold it for a minute," Uno said, turning the volume on the T.V. up.

"This is Destiny Black reporting to you live with breaking news. We have yet two killings to add to the city's Astronomically Heinous 152 for the year.

As you can see behind me, the police have the entire area taped off. This is the result of a call from a neighbor reporting that this house had a really bad smell coming from it. When police arrived, they found a woman tied to a chair beheaded and a man brutally stabbed. They don't have any leads at the moment but are diligently searching. Now to the Chief of police who is live from Downtown Destiny Black, signing off.

"Hello, I'm Police Chief Cartel. The city of Indianapolis has been like a war zone with all the killings. We also have drugs flooding the streets and I want to promise the community that I'm going to lock up everybody that has any part in any of this. With the help of the F.B.I., we will find all of you responsible for turning our city into a battleground. Crime is at an all-time high and I want my streets safe again. So this is your last warning! Thank you

"Damn! Shit about to get really hot now," Nasty said.

"I say y'all need to pack up and leave the city for a while, that will be the smartest move. Y'all just heard the man and the Feds is nothing to play with," Ant said.

All y'all niggas have to do is give me some money to invest so y'all money can be clean. Feel me?" Ant said offering the men an answer to the question he knew they were asking themselves. But regardless, I gotta get up out of here," Ant said giving everyone a dap.

Ant, I'm not worried about the Feds, Fat D said, so I'm good on the money tip.

When Ant opened the front door, he ran into Breezy." What's good with you?" Ant asked.

"Shit comin' to see how Uno is holding up. Is he here?" Breezy asked, looking at Ant.

"Yea, gon' up."

When Breezy walked into the room, everybody looked her way." What's up? Fellas." Breezy greeted with a smile on her face before sitting down next to Uno.

"What's good? They all said at the same time. "We are going to get up out of here' Nasty said as they all got up to give Uno a brotherly hug.

Once everybody was gone, Uno just sat there quietly looking at Breezy. He didn't know if it was because of the gravity of his heartbreak or what but at that moment, he began to see her in a different light.

He knew missing Breezy probably wouldn't be proper or good for business. But Dayum, she was really that bitch. Uno remembers the first time he introduced her to the homies, how Fat-D's mouth hit his chest and a smile touched a corner of his mouth.

But Breezy was colder than the north pole. She always stayed dipped, wearing the shit out of the nicest designer pantsuits. Her hair stayed buttered like toast, and her sexy ass lips reminded Uno of da wettest candy paint he had ever seen.

From where Uno was sitting, it was like his nostril was being teased by her wonderful aroma. He didn't know what her fragrance was called, but it should be 'lick me all over' 'cause that's what it made Uno want to do.

Breezy had crossed her legs and was now rocking her pedicure's foot that was clad in a peep toe red bottom to tune only she could hear. Fingers and toes nails were all adorned with a diamond design and all Uno could think about is putting them in his mouth and sucking on them one by one real slowly until Breezy's back arched in pleasure. He could imagine her pretty little light-skinned fingers wrapped around his pole caressing it, and stroking it.

The craziest thang about Breezy was that she wasn't the type of woman that only affected a man's little head, she affected the big one too. Uno liked that Breezy could hold a conversation with him because most females couldn't because they weren't on shit. And on top of always knowing what to say and went to say, it seemed like she stayed checking for Uno.

Breezy parked her car a block away from the address Duffle Bag gave her. She and Uno slid out of the car and quietly walked up the street and through the yard until they reached the front door.

Breezy tried the knob to see if it was unlocked and to their surprise, it opened. Breezy pulled her .9mm out and Uno did the same with his .45 cal. They quietly moved through the house. Hearing movement upstairs, they both took the steps one at a time. Uno slowly crept up on the door where the noise was coming from and kicked it open. Inside, they saw a man in the bed stirring from sleep.

"What the fuck is going on?" The man asked jumping up. Breezy let a shot off in his head knocking him back on the bed and to sleep but this time, it would be forever.

Uno trained his gun on the mark, the same woman Duffle Bag had a picture of. Just as she fixed her mouth to scream, Uno grabbed her. Now I'm going to ask you something and if you don't answer right, you will end up like… Uno said pointing to the bed.

"Where is the hard drive?" Breezy asked, walking up to the woman.

"It's in the safe behind the family picture on the wall. The code is 8-3-3-11" the woman said crying.

Uno grabbed his knife off his waist and lunged it into the woman's neck three times. After Breezy grabbed the hard drive, they exited the house the same way they came.

Dropping Uno off, Breezy went to her house she was renting out North. Walking through the door, she quickly removed her clothes and jumped in the shower. Instead of letting her mind wander like usual, she solely focused on washing her body thoroughly. Minutes later, she jumped out.

Breezy oiled her body up and tried to make up her mind about what she wanted to wear. After grabbing a black pantsuit with some Choo heels to match, she got dressed.

"I love you uncle, it's done," she texted Duffle Bag.

Chapter 26

Tezzy, LR, Fat-D and Nasty sat on the spot counting the money they just collected from the streets. The flip had been good, and everybody was eating like KINGS from the top all the way down to the bottom.

"How much is that?" Nasty asked Tezzy throwing a big stack in the bag.

"It's 3.5" he stated.

"Ok, put that to the side. That bag is the plugs," LR said.

All you heard were bills flipping through the money machine and occasional coughing from the potent loud pack they were smoking. After the money machine counted it, Tezzy checked it, then LR made sure it was right.

"We have to put another 1.5 to the side for the plug." Uno will be meeting him in the next week, so we have to be ready. And we are about to up our shipment since we are going to be serving the whole city and the surrounding ones," LR said passing the blunt to Nasty.

After we finish doing this, we are going to have a little get-together on Roach, so make sure all the runners and workers are around cause I'm going to give them something for working so hard," Fat-D said counting a stack of money. Also, tell Uno to come through.

"You know Uno isn't about to be hanging out with any runners and we are not either. We have too much money to be sitting around them little niggas. It's good to show our face but that ain't nothing. Plus Uno has been chilling out ever since Feds hit the city," LR said."

"Man, tell him he is coo, they are not on shit right now," Fat-D said.

"How do you know they are not on anything?" LR asked looking at Fat-D in the eyes.

"I just know bro, damn, he is good," Fat-D said feeling some type of way about LR being on his back.

Breezy pulled up to Uno's crib and he jumped in. She pulled her Benz into traffic as if she was in a hurry. Uno leaned over to turn up Breezy's radio, but she slapped his hand away. "Sit back and chill," she said, looking at Uno.

"You don't know shit about Boosie anyway," Uno said, sucking his teeth.

As Breezy drove, Uno ogled from her nice legs all the way up to her sexy lips. "Damn, look at them thighs," he said to himself. Her legs were toned nicely which told Uno she worked out.

"What are you looking at?" Breezy asked.

"Shid, at yo' nice body and while we on da topic I was thinking about how you'd fit as good in my life, as you are in that tight ass pantsuit," Uno said. Breezy just smiled.

"Sure," Breezy said, turning down the music."

"For starters, why don't you have a man, and secondly why do I only see you in pantsuits even tho you look sexy in them?" Uno said, licking his lips.

"Well, for the first question, Shid, I was with a dude for ten years and he played me by cheating, so I'm taking a break from relationships. And for the second question, Shid, I love my pantsuits," she said winking at him before laughing.

"Damn, this bitch is packed," Breez said out loud as she and Uno hopped out of the Benz and headed towards the entrance. At the front door stood a big bouncer who Uno had hired on his size alone.

"Yo Buff, what's up?" Uno asked, giving him a brotherly hug.

117

The two walked into Auntie Bugg's and were immediately treated like royalty. Uno looked like a million bucks. His wrist, neck and pinky ring looked like Christmas lights as they bounced off the walls like mini disco balls.

Walking through the club, every female mugged Breezy, 'cause they wanted to be in her position on Uno's arm.

"I see you stunt like old money Bossman Uno with that bad lady on your side," the DJ shouted as Uno and Breezy got to the V.I.P. tables.

"Let's get a few bottles over here," Uno ordered as he listened to the music pounding through the speakers.

"Why did he call you Bossman Uno" Breezy leaned over to ask Uno.

"Cause this is my place. I named it after the best auntie in the world," Uno said.

"Breezy just sat back listening to the music and watched Uno turn down female after female.

"I saw you from across the room sitting over her chilling and had to know if you here with someone." a light-skinned man asked Breezy. Breezy saw this as an opportunity to put up a boundary between her and Uno.

"Yea, I'm here with a friend, but you can sit," Breezy said looking at Uno and seeing the look in his eyes.

"My name is Cheese," the man said, extending his hand.

"It's nice to meet you Mr. Cheese," Breezy said, shaking his hand while looking him in the eye.

"So why would a woman let a handsome man like yourself out of the house?" Breezy asked.

"I don't have any woman in my life," Cheese said.

While Breezy and Cheese talked the night away, Uno just sat back and let Breezy enjoy her night out. Uno knew Breezy could see he was shitty that she got one up on him but he wasn't tripping because he was a Boss.

"Well, can I get a number?" Cheese asked Breezy cause I'm about to head to the crib.

"Ok," Breezy said, locking her number in his phone. I promise to call Cheese said walking off.

As Breezy sat back in her seat, she saw two Mexican looking at her and Uno. The two men exchanged words before they started walking towards their table. Breezy grabbed her 9mm while hitting Uno in the leg under the table.

Uno looked up and saw the two men coming towards them with non-threatening body language, but it was their eyes that gave away their true intent to kill.

Jumping up, Breezy let off two shots hitting one in the head, dropping him. Uno bumped three shots in the other gunman's chest, and he joined his partner on the other side.

"Let's go. We are out of here" Uno said, grabbing Breezy's hand and exiting out the back way right to the car. Uno hopped behind the wheel and pulled out of the lot.

"Jimmy's bitch ass has to go," Uno yelled, hitting the palm of his hand with his fist. He was tired of the back-and-forth shit, so now it was time to eliminate any last competitors and all remaining enemies.

Chapter 27

LR, Lil E, Tezzy and Nasty pulled up to a white house on Roach. It was a lot going on out there but out of everything they saw, they saw their crew getting money, so they were all happy.

Hopping out and walking into the house, they were all greeted with smoke, loud music and many pairs of nipples. As they made their way through the house, everybody wanted to shake their hands and give them hugs. They were all Bosses and everyone in town knew it.

Walking to the back room, they entered it, shut and locked the door so no one could get inside. LR hit the light switch in and they all watched as the floor came up to reveal the safe. LR hit the combination and the safe popped open. Grabbing the stacks of money out and putting them in bags, LR handed them to Nasty.

"Can you take these to your safe on Edgemont, Nasty?" LR asked.

"Yea, coo, me and Tezzy will be back in a few minutes." Fat D just hit and said he is right around the corner," Nasty said.

Walking out of the room, they say the house was full of people and the party was jumping. LR knew he shouldn't have been there but got right in the mix of things, joining in on the crowd's chant, "Ain't no parties like a West side party cuz a West side party don't stop!" LR yelled.

Fifteen minutes later, Nasty and Tezzy were turning back down Roach but Nasty slammed on the brakes stopping his Lexus Coupe instantly. They saw the Drug Enforcement Agents rushing the house from every direction.

Kicking down the door, the agents rushed inside the house. The music was so loud, nobody even heard the door coming down.

"Indianapolis Police Department get down now! LR and Lil E were slammed to the floor and cuffed quickly.

"Damn bitch ass cracker pig muthafucka" LR growled angrily.

"Shut the fuck up before I hurt you," One of the agents said hating the ground the drug lord walks on. "We are going to take you and all your friends down one by one if we have to." LR just smiled at him.

From down the block, Nasty and Tezzy pulled out their phones and broke them in half while shaking their heads. Pulling off, Nasty lit a blunt and they rode through the city clearing their minds.

Ant laid Lauren on the bed while sucking on her nipples before working his way down to her love box. Grabbing his head, Lauren pushed him into her pussy. Ant licked inside of her pussy and tongue kissed her clit aggressively until he started moaning really loud and couldn't take it anymore and she started to cum all over his face. Licking her all up before flipping her on her stomach, Ant began by rubbing his dick up and down her ass crack and pussy. Entering her, Ant started off really slow so she could get use to the dick and once she did, he started trashing her from the back while shutting his eyes as the feeling of her tight pussy walls blessed his dick.

Turning her over on her back again, Ant put her legs on his shoulders before he slid his dick inside with ease. He began pounding her pussy with hard and long strokes.

"Damn, Ant...I loved you beat this pussy up, give me all the dick please" Lauren moaned." "Baby, I'm about to cum again Lauren cried," shaking. After seeing Lauren cum all over his dick again, Ant couldn't hold back. Lauen wasn't just any bitch. Ant loved her, so there was no need to pull out, so Ant just kept on pumping until his dick finally erupted filling Lauren with the hot fluid of his cum.

Falling on the bed, Ant laid back and Lauren put her head on his heaving chest and turned the TV on.

"I'm Erica White reporting for Channel 12 news. We are here tonight on Roach Street on the city's West Side, where there's been a record-breaking drug indictment. The IMPD with the help of the FBI had apprehended over 35 people most of who are involved with the Notorious West Side Family in this major drug bust. As of now, names have been released to the public. We will have more information for you later at 11 o'clock. Remember you heard it here first. Back to you Brian.

Ant hopped up and tried to call Uno but didn't get an answer. Not one to jump to conclusions, Ant figured his Lil Bro was prolly in some pussy somewhere so he shot him a text to make sure he was coo.

"Damn, I hope Lil Bro wasn't over there," Ant said to himself. Going through his contacts on his phone, Ant called one of the police he had on the payroll.

"Boss," the police said, picking up on the first ring.

"They locked up a lot of my people. I need you to find out who they have and what they are looking for," Ant said before hanging up without getting a response.

Chapter 28

LR and Lil E stood in front of the judge with their heads up and chest out. From the jump, both men knew what they had signed up for, so when the judge denied them bonds, there were no signs of it affecting them whatsoever.

But no matter how they looked on the outside, it was a pure contradiction because even with being hit with conspiracy to commit murder, money laundering, drug trafficking, and a gang enhancement, they still felt the sting of being shot down by the judge. As far as the lower members of WSF, their bonds were all set at $20,000 each.

Every police in Indiana was looking for Uno because an arrest warrant was issued for him and he was labeled as armed and dangerous.

Later on that night, still sitting in intake waiting to be transferred to the county, LR and the crew just sat around joking and talking like they weren't looking at football numbers. People were playing cards, rapping and talking about what they were on the street doing.

When the night started setting, the WSF went to a corner to chop it up between themselves because nine out of ten times when they got to the county, they would all be in different units.

"I wonder why Fat-D didn't show up, he had just called to say he was down the street. Then the police kicked in the door. That don't look right" Lil E said, "That shit look fucked up" he kept going.

"Y'all need to shut that shit up, my nigga has been down with us for the longest," LR said without looking up,

"I ain't saying snitches but Lil E is right, plus we heard the police say someone gave them information," one of the workers chimed."

"Y'all need not to worry. Y'all will be home soon with y'all dick in some pussy," LR said. "So be coo"

Ant had been so worried about Uno that he couldn't sleep. Calling the police, he has on the payroll again, Ant waited to hear his voice.

"What have you heard? Ant asked as soon as he heard the other end pick up."

"Well, they locked up a few of your people in the crew. All their bonds are set at $20,00 each but they denied LR and Lil E bond. You need to get a hold of your brother to let him know that every office in the city is looking for him as we speak. If you asked me it's in his best interest on the front and the back end to turn himself in. And Ant, I'm not just saying this because I wear this wack ass badge either.

"I'll make sure I let them know," Ant stated, traces of pain lingering in his voice.

"Oh, and Ant, the F.E.D'S are looking around in town."

Breezy lay on her bed wearing nothing but a thong staring at her phone waiting to see if Uno would call her. The only thing on her mind was if Uno was safe because he'd been on the news all night. Breezy kept thinking about Uno until she heard her phone ring. She looked at her phone and didn't know the number.

"What's up?" She answered.

"What's up Sexy? Are you busy? Uno asked.

"No, not at the moment. why? What's up?" she asked, smiling at herself.

"Open the door then," he said hanging up. She hopped up quickly and ran to open the door. Uno walked in and looked at Breezy in a thong and licked his lips.

"Damn Breezy, you're wearing that thong," Uno said, slapping her ass as he walked past. Remembering she only had on a thong, she walked to her room to put on some pants. As she walked past, she put a little extra in it because she knew he was looking.

A few minutes later, Breezy came back in with some sweatpants and a t-shirt on." So, what's up?" She asked, sitting next to him on the sofa.

"Man, I know you've been watching the news. I have to get my people out of there before they can build a case, feel me?" Uno said.

"Yea I feel you. Do you need me to do anything, cause I'm here for you 100%? I have lawyers and bail bondsmen on speed dial, legitimate accounts, and cribs in three different cities if you try to lay low," Breezy said, grabbing Uno's hand.

"Naw, I'm coo but I do need you to go with me to meet this lawyer and I need you to bond out my people. I will have the money for you after we meet the lawyer" Uno said.

"Well, you been on ya mind all" Breezy said.

"Really, Uno asked, looking at her with a grin.

"Not like that" she smiled back, but Uno could tell if he wanted to pursue her, he would have good luck; she was his type of woman in every aspect also.

"Are you hungry?" I can cook you something before I go to bed," Breezy said standing up.

"I'm a good Wifey," Uno said. And I'm staying the night."

"What do you call me?" she asked.

"Wifey. What do you have a problem with?" Uno asked, looking enlightened.

"Naw, it's good daddy," Breezy said walking off laughing.

Chapter 29

Uno and Breezy walked inside Desiree and Amaya's Sister of the Law Office. Walking up to the reception desk, Uno asked the assistant to speak with Desiree or Amaya.

The assistant walked to the back for a few minutes and returned with a light skin woman following her.

"Hello, my name is Desiree'. May I help you?"

"Uno shook her waiting hand before getting straight to the point." I need to hire you and your sister ASAP. A few of my people told me you were the best at what you do, so I know my money would be well spent." Uno said, lifting the duffle bag.

"Well, follow me to my office so we can talk more," Desiree said eyeing the bag that looked to weigh a ton. After Desiree lowered her small petite frame behind his desk, she followed the tone Uno set earlier and got straight to business. "Now y'all know my service isn't cheap," Desiree said.

Uno smiled. "Money isn't an issue. You name the price and you will have it, so how much for you to get started?"

"Well, I need $20,000 just to look at the cases," Desiree informed.

"I also have two brothers they denied bonds on. They have been charged with Conspiracy to commit murder, Money laundering, Drug trafficking, and Gang enhancement," Uno said.

"Since it's two brothers, I will charge you $35,000 just to look at their case and another $75,000 to take on the case," Desiree said.

"So, here's the $55,000 and an extra $35,000 because I'm going to need you also," Uno said, laying stacks on her desk. Plus, I have a warrant out for my arrest, so I need you to assist me in turning myself in so if you can make a few phone calls, we would be ready to go in, in a few days, Uno said, laying another stack of money on her desk.

"Ant, I need you and Nasty to go see the plug, because I'm turning myself in tomorrow," Uno said. "Also, I need you to make sure Nasty feeds the streets. I'm going to hand everything over to Nasty, Tezzy and Lil E. Breezy is going with me to turn myself in and after that, she will fly out of town for a while." Uno said, looking at Ant.

"Well, Nasty will make sure everything is under control," Ant said, patting Uno on the back. "But I have one question to ask you Breezy. Where in the hell did you come from?" Ant said, looking at her skeptically.

"What do you mean?" she asked unfoundedly.

"What chu mean, what I mean? Never in my life have I ever seen you or ever heard of you for that matter. And as long as I have been running these streets, I know every soul— whoever has any type of real weight or made any major paper. So, I ask again, where in the hell did you come from, Breezy?

"Well, calm down my dude, my uncle knows Uno, so they clicked up to do some work and I ended up linking up with both ofb them," she answered, sipping her drink.

"Ok then," Ant said, content with her answer for now.

"Big bro, her uncle is Duffle Bag," Uno said getting ready to leave. "You ready Wifey?" Uno asked surprising Ant with the name he called her.

A few days later, Uno and Breezy walked into the City-County building with Uno's lawyers in tow. The lawyers had to do a lot of fighting with the prosecutor on the case but they came to an understanding. The prosecutor finally ended up agreeing to let everybody out but LR.

Desiree filed a Motion of Discovery and got right to the point. LT Spell was pissed because after all the   work he had put in, the F.E.D. s was taking over the case.

Chapter 30

Inside the gray brick and stained white walls of the Federal Courthouse located in downtown Indianapolis, Murrell "Uno" Brandon and Rodney "LR" Brew were on trial for their life.

Uno and LR sat calmly beside their female lawyers, Desiree Star and Amaya Star. Uno and LR sat calm and relaxed in their black Gucci suits with black gators waiting on the jury to come back.

The WSF organization supposedly led by Uno and LR is responsible for the murders of just about anyone who stepped in their path to the top. The government wanted the two put away for the rest of their life, and they didn't want anything or anyone to get in the way of that. The two were considered the biggest thing that came out of Indianapolis in the last 15 years. The organization was feared by many.

Uno and LR had been charged with racketeering, and conspiracy to purchase and distribute more than 1,000 kilograms. For years, the authorities tried to link them to the hundreds of bodies that had appeared and disappeared along the path of violence. The type of viciousness Uno and LR was releasing on the streets quickly earned them a seat at the top of FBI's most wanted list. As far as the DEA and the ATF were concerned, there wasn't anybody more dangerous walking the streets of Indianapolis.

Uno glanced around the courtroom at all the people that were crowded in. The faces of family members, friends, enemies, victims, officers, reporters, and ghosts from the past all were sitting waiting to see the outcome of the biggest trial Indianapolis had seen.

Working her way up from the bottom of her class to become the best known criminal defense lawyer in the country Desiree stood 5 feet and 2 inches tall but when she stood in the courtroom, it was as if she was a giant. She gave respect and demanded it in return, and she had established a great deal of rapport among her colleagues. She knew when the right moment was to inflect her voice. This was the biggest case of her career and she knew the stakes were high but no matter what, she made sure to bring her A-game.

It had been a long four months of exhibits, photographs, witnesses, objections and explanations. Every day seemed longer than the one before. Today was the final day and the verdict would be read.

Judge Melvin B. Webster leaned back in his seat giving his back rest for the first time that day. Taking a deep breath Mr. Webster closed his eyes momentarily, wondering where he took a turn at arriving at this point in his life.

Mexican by birth, born to immigrant parents who made their first home as a family in the United States (California), he had seen so much during his 65 years on earth. His face was clean, with a thin mustache and a bald head.

Serving as a federal judge for nearly twenty years, he had seen things change. He had power and intelligence, sure about himself. From the smallest to the biggest criminal couldn't escape his gravity.

This case had a great deal of attention on it from the press as well as from behind closed doors where a lot of powerful people silently had their hands involved.

This case was about much more than Murrell "Uno" Brandon and Rodney "LR" Brew.

Judge Webster looked around the courtroom at the many faces.

The courtroom fell silent before Judge Webstar could get his hands on his gravel. It was like the Judge and the courtroom had an understanding.

"Mr. Foreman, did the jury reach a final verdict?" Judge Webster asked, clearing his throat.

"Yes we have, your honor," the foreman said as he stood. The bailiff then walked over and was handed a folded piece of paper. Everyone's eyes in the courtroom followed the paper from the jury box to the Judge's hand.

The Judge leaned down to grab the paper from the bailiff. He glanced at the paper and folded it back up.

"Mr. Brandon and Mr. Brew, will you please stand for the reading of your verdict?" Judge Webster said looking over at Desiree and Amaya.

Chapter 31

The beginning, Indianapolis, fifteen years earlier...

"Chow time five minutes! Chow time five minutes!" The % yelled over the intercom in the dorm.

Getting up off his bunk, Uno grabbed his morning hygiene and headed to get ready.

"You walking over there with me cuz?" Uno asked.

"What?" "Hell naw! You know I'm not fucking with that trash shit and I don't understand why you keep going with all this food in this room?" Baby J replied flipping through some new pictures Uno received the night before from Big Dawg or Any. He was looking at all the new fashion.

Enthusiastic was the reason Baby J paced the room all night. After spending his last two birthdays in the State Boy school, today the state was releasing Baby J before his fifteen birthday. The state was letting people go home that only had a few months left on their sentence.

A week ago, Baby J was called out to his counselor's office and was informed that the state wanted him released. Ever since that day, Baby J's mind has been in overdrive thinking about everything possible.

Imagining his mom and Granny's cooking, Baby J licked his lips.

Uno opens his box to put his hygiene back and to check his fade in the mirror. Late last night, he had Baby J fade him up so the waves in his hair did a 360 around his head.

"Damn, cuz at least walk with a nigga!" Uno yelled from the mirror.

"Aight, nigga you got that!" Baby J replied while getting off his bunk.

Uno smiled as he watched Baby J walk up to him.

"Give Big Cuz some love," Baby J said with his arms open. Honestly, both of them were emotional and hurt. They were going to miss each other like hell. After sharing the same room for the last two years, the two had grown closer than they were on the streets. They shared a lot of the same interests. Some nights, they would stay up talking about some of the trouble they use to be on out in the world.

Uno and Baby J were second cousins. Baby J, his mother and brother Bird use to stay with Uno's mother. It was known throughout the boy school that if you fucked with one, you had to deal with both and dudes already knew what that meant; Trouble. Even tho both of them knew how to throw their hands, Baby J was more laid back whereas Uno constantly stayed putting his hands on someone. It got so bad that Baby J already knew when he stepped out the gates, Uno was going to turn the heat up on niggas. At 5'3 toting around 175 pounds, Uno was good-looking, brown-skinned with a fade he had Baby J cut once a week. Where Baby J toted around 190, standing at 5'6, dark-skinned with long braids.

Baby J gathered all his belongings while Uno finished doing him. He smiled to himself while taking down the rest of his pictures. He had his mind set that if his family wasn't on the same page as him then they could kick rocks and that went for anyone.

"What time Cuz 'pose to be here?" Uno asked.

"I think around 9 a.m.," Baby J replied.

"So, Cuz, are you going to holla at ol' girl for me?"

Uno inquired looking at Baby J move around the room.

Baby J smiled. "I'ma swing pass there after I walk with you," he said, grabbing Uno around the shoulders as they walked and talked.

Creased down from head to toe in state-issued, both swagged to the chow hall like they were dressed to go on a visit. While walking up the walkway, both exchanged farewell daps with all the dudes they knew or respected.

When they stepped inside the chow hall, Uno grabbed his food, while Baby J just opted for apple juice. Sitting down in their usual spot in the back, Baby J briefed Uno on any and everything he needed to know about the dealings he had done. For the past year and a half, they had the boy school cracking with weed and tobacco.

"Listen, that nigga C-murder from my way owe me hundred-fifty dollars, Yammy owes three-hundred-dollars, Rob and Lil Jay trying to grab a few grams of Loud, Anthony Larossa and Cody from out south get a QP and a few cups of tobacco. Them two already paid last night. It's a little over a pound of weed and 2 pounds of tobacco in the spot and that should hold you up till my brother or yours holla at ol'girl out there," Baby J said looking around the chow hall.

Uno just smiled as he listened to Baby J. It was always about business with him.

"Damn, I'ma miss you, cuz," Uno said.

"Nigga, you touch down real soon. Just lay back and stack some money up. I'ma have shit popping by the time you come home. Plus you know I only have two months of papers."

"Shit about to be popping. My fifteenth birthday is coming up, so I'm going to do it big," Baby J said with a smirk on his face.

After they departed from the chow hall, Uno headed to bust a few moves before he had to go into school for his test, while Baby J swagged to his counselor Ms. Long's office to say goodbye.

Knock … Knock … Knock Baby J pushed open the door. Ms. Long's face lit up like a Christmas tree when she saw Baby J's face just standing there.

Remembering a year and a half ago when Baby J and Uno walked into her office looking all fresh.

Flashbacks of when her, Bird, and Ant went to school together played in her mind like a movie. Kids in school picked on her but Bird and Ant were the only ones that came to her aid, and from there on, they built a friendship. Tears threatened to fall from her eyes as she remembered how the two were always there to comfort her when they saw her crying in the hallways.

"I need you to get at cuz," Baby J said

"Anything for y'all, just let me know and it's done," She said, shaking her head at how much Baby J looked like his cousin Ant.

"Look, the fam is going to pull up on you a few times for Uno, please make sure he gets his shit," Baby J said. I know you to Ant and Bird that when I or Uno got released, you would stop bringing in the stuff but, you know how family is to us! So really, either of us can just stop the show, feel me?" Baby J replied.

"Okay, I'm going to hit the family on my lunch break. You just make sure you don't come back and I will see," Ms. Long said, pushing Baby J out of her office.

***

"Mr. Williams, report to R & R!" Baby J heard over the intercom, as he headed back to the unit to grab up his stuff.

"Damn, nigga, you act like you don't wanna go to the crib taking all day and shit?" Uno said, walking into the room.

Baby J just smiled. "Cuz if I didn't take my time, you would be hit."

"So, I'm good then?" Uno asked.

"Fo' sho!' Baby J replied

After giving out dap, Baby J looked around the dorm and yelled. "See y'all on the other side!" Then he and Uno took off towards R & R.

During the walk, Baby J explained to Uno that he had to come up with a drop for Ms. Long. Baby J wore a smile on his face making him look like the Kool-Aid man. So many dudes came out to see him off. Even a lot of the women officers were out there waving. By the time they hit R & R, they got a little emotional.

"Love cuz," Baby J said, giving Uno a hug, "I'll see you soon."

Ten minutes later, Baby J was being escorted to the front gate with all his teeth showing. It felt so good to be dressed in something other than the boy school issues.

"Look at my baby!" was the first thing he heard when the gates opened up. Baby J's mom was running towards him with her arms open and tears coming down her face. His brother walked up to get his love as well. After a few minutes, they loaded back into Bird F-250 while Baby J looked at the boy's school walls thinking that would never be him again.

"Let's get up outta here!" Baby J said.

Chapter 32

Fast forward 2 months...

Big Dawg's Mercedes-Benz crusade through the streets as Uno twisted and turned all in his seat trying to see who was who. He was amazed at how Indianapolis looked like a whole new city. Stores and new buildings were everywhere.

You can tell I have been gone for two and a half years, he thought, as they passed a block that looked like a car show. Uno couldn't believe all the cars they passed were foreign sitting on rims. When he looked harder, he noticed a few nobodies and some females were even riding in their cute little cars.

Damn, it's niggas my age out riding. I'm about to be 14, I have to step my game up, fuck shining off my brothers, Uno thought to himself shaking his head and smiling while rubbing his hands together at the same time.

Being locked up did something to Uno, so he took the last two months to better himself and the situation for those around him. Taking what he knew, what he was taught and saw, he and Baby J took over the boy school which he was going to do to the streets.

When Big Dawg whipped his Mercedes down his mother's block, the first thing he saw was a banner that read "Welcome Home." All Uno could do was smile and shake his head. His mom's house looks really good on the outside and he remembers her telling him she did a little something.

"Damn!" Uno said, staring at all his family standing in front of the house. As soon as he stepped out of the car, the family started cheering. Giving out love and daps, Uno made his way through. Uno was in the rush to see one person, his best friend. She was one of the few people that held him down with pictures, letters, money, and phone calls. That made him love her even more. Even tho they both were single, he knew he would pursue a relationship, but he wanted to step his game up because she dated a few older guys and he wanted her to look at him like the boss he was.

Uno shook his head as he saw Punkin standing there looking good. She looks better than the last time he saw her. Punkin's mom drove her up to see him one time, after that, it flooded through the boy school that Uno had a girl from Everybody Hate Chris in the visiting room.

The whole time Uno was walking toward her, she was doing her own inspection of Uno. She smiled at how fine Uno had gotten. It's been over a year since they last saw each other. His arms and Chest got bigger and his hair even was wavey. Making her way down his body, her eyes made their way down to his dick print. Licking her lips as she made her way back up his body.

"Look at yourself looking all edible," Punkin said as the two hugged and kissed.

As everybody made it into the house, Punkin handed him his chain and ring that Big Dawg and Ant gave her to hold for him. Putting the chain on and sliding the ring on his finger, he kissed it.

A few hours later, the whole block was in full swing. The men all drunk, played cards and talked about the streets. The kids played among themselves while the women cooked and did the won thang. Uno and Punkin sat in a chair off in a corner talking, Uno looked up and smiled at everything that was going on.

"Let me holla at you for a hot second," Big Dawg told Uno.

"I'll be back bae," Uno said following Beg Dawg to the porch where Ant, Bird and Slow stood sipping on beers.

Everyone had a big Kool-Aid smile on their faces when they stepped onto the porch.

"Look at you, bro!" Big Dawg opened his arms and the two hugged.

"Man, this shit is crazy around here bro, everything changed," Uno reasoned as they released each other.

"Where my cuz at Bird,' Uno asked Baby J's brother.

"That ill' nigga out post turning the heat up on them young niggas," Bird said.

"Let him know I'm home," Uno replied.

"Here," Big Dawg said, handing Uno a stack of money. "That's five grand, put it up," he said.

"Thanks bro," I really appreciate y'all keeping me and Baby J books laced and handling that other thing for us," Uno said to all.

'So what's your plan," Big Dawg asked, staring Uno in the eyes to see if he was going to lie to him about what he was going to do.

"Get a feel of this shit and try to get me some pussy from Punkin," Uno said with a smile on his face thinking about how he'd be her first.

Everybody on the porch shook their heads.

"Have a seat," Ant said, pushing out a chair for him to sit in.

"Okay, these streets ain't sweet, you have to take the good with the bad and you have to be a cold muthafucka. It's different walking this life and only knowing about the life, feel me!" Big Dawg said.

"Hell naw, if everything was perfect, you would never learn and you would never grow," Bird said, puffing on a blunt now.

"Lil Bro, I want you to go to school and say fuck all the other shit, but I know your lil badass is going to do what you want to do, so I'm going to drop this on you. Always be your own leader, if you pull that pistol, use it. And most importantly, we are not impressed about a nigga killing someone, we are impressed by the nigga that's taking care of his family. Build your own shit," Ant said.

"If you build your own circle, you would go to the top. I see a lion in you and I know you are hungry, so eat and respect; blessed is he who expects nothing for he shall never be disappointed," Slow said.

Every last one of them took turns dropping jewels on Uno. Big Dawg grabbed Uno by the shoulders and gave him some last-minute jewels.

"Everybody out for self and tryna outdo the next person. These little niggas don't want to put in sweat, blood and tears in this shit. The only thing they want is a handout. Some of these little niggas are the same ones that you grew up with. Whoever has the dope and money, no matter if they rats or not. everybody wants to ride they dicks," Big Dawg said. "Make sure you plan for your life. Remember, life is a gamble, but you have a better chance than these other niggas out here," Big Dawg said pointing at his brain. "Your mind can take you anywhere you wanna go. The more you train your mind, the more it grows because it's a muscle!" I know you have a lot going on up there," Big Dawg said pointing to Uno's head, "but one thing for sure is that if you do go out in the streets causing hell, nothing better not land on my momma's doorstep because then you going to have to see us.

***

The next morning around 9 a.m. Uno got dressed and grabbed his keys to his old scooter his mom put up for him when he got sent to boy school. Headed out the door to the mall, he wanted to be one of the few people there when the doors opened. Walking towards his scooter on the side of the house, he spotted an all-white Jag slowly coming down the block.

Who the hell is this riding like this? He thought to himself as he started backing up towards the house. Uno stood back on the porch with a mug on his face. The driver stopped and backed up in front of the house, let down the window, and showed his face.

"Uno, is that you?" I heard you came home yesterday." Tryna makes out the voice. Uno slowly moved towards the car to put a face with the voice.

"It's me, nigga ... Man-Man!"

Uno's eyes popped out of his face. When Uno got sent to boy school, Man-Man was a dirty, scared dude. Now Man-Man was riding a Jag, draped in ice, golds in his mouth and sporting the newest threads and he was only one year older than Uno. Uno smiled on the inside because no matter what Man-Man has going on, he will always be that scared dude he knew growing up. He also didn't like Man-Man because he used to talk to Punkin and when she didn't give up the pussy he kicked her to the curb.

"Damn, nigga, you done got big!" Man-Man said, stepping out of the car and giving Uno some fake love.

Uno's eyes kept wandering over Man-Man's expensive jewelry and Man-Man saw it, so he kept twisting his ring.

"This bitch out here doing it for real," Uno thought.

"Check dog, I know how it is when you are just coming home, so here's a little something to get you by," Man-Man said handing him twenty hundred dollar bills. Next, Man-Man wrote down his number. "I know you gon' to chill for a while but hit me up if you need a job, and by the looks of that old ass scooter, I know you are going to be calling. I remember when you pulled that old thing out, the hood thought you were the shit," he added before hopping back in the car and honking his horn.

Uno stood there in astonishment with Man-Man's number in his hand: "Hit me if you need a job?" he said to himself, then crumbled the paper and toss it in the street.

The mall was packed early, but then again, he heard the new Jordans were coming out, plus it was a Friday. For the next few hours, Uno balled his heart out. It felt so good to be home. As he swagged from store to store, he saw people he hasn't seen in years. Females were throwing their numbers at him and he was loving it.

After chopping down his food, he headed over to Hat World to grab him a few hats. While he searched the wall for something he liked, he smiled when he spotted his nigga, Nasty's cousin, Ashley looking at some female hats on the other side of the store. Looking at Ashley's fat ass, Uno couldn't do anything but shake his head. He's been tryna fuck Ashley since he met her but she always blew him off saying he was too young.

"Ashely, what's good?" Uno asked with a smirk.

"Oh shit," Ashley said, lost for words at how fine Uno got.

"You know your cousin only has a few weeks left up top," he told her.

Ashley hadn't heard anything, he said she was too busy feeling him out. Taking a piece of paper and pen out, she wrote down her number and address for him.

"Nigga, you know what time it is with me. Hit me up when you get yourself together," Ashley said, strutting off with extra in her walk.

By the time Uno arrived at his scooter, he was tired. He was about to throw his bag inside the department under the seat when a black Cadillac truck pulled up and someone yelled his name.

"Uno! Long time no see! The driver said, hopping out.

"Baby J, what's good Big Cuz?" Uno said smiling.

"It's me in the flesh! Baby J replied, showing a mouth full of VV's at the top and the bottom.

"Look at you, all iced out and shit," Uno laughed. Baby J came home running. For the last few months, he has been turning up the heat on the niggas out post-pushing weed.

Uno noticed Baby J eyes were slated.

"You out here doing yo' thang I see?" Uno commented.

"You know my name stamped with the best out here!" Baby J bragged. "Hop in and fuck with me for a little while.

After locking the scooter back up, Uno hopped in with Baby J and they cruised around the city passing blunts back and forth while Baby J stop to make stings along the way.

"This some good shit! What are you hitting for? Uno asked.

"You little cuz so you can get it the same price I got it for," Baby J said.

***

Ashely opened the front door wearing nothing but a pair of red pumps on. Her perfume slap him in the face as he stood with his mouth open as she stepped to the side. Once Uno was inside her parents' house, she didn't waste any time getting down to business.

Uno was fresh out, and she wanted the dick before he started passing it out. She walked Uno to the love seat and pushed him into it. Bending over in front of him, she started fingering her pussy in front of his face. Uno's dick grew the more she played and moaned. After cumming all over her fingers she put them in her mouth and sucked all her cum off. No one would have known Ashley birth two kids because her genetics looked like she worked out or ran track. She had a few stretch marks, beside that, her body was tight. Ashley still look the same as he remembers. The only thing is that she got taller, and thicker and her hair was longer.

"Is this what you been wanting?" Ashley asked Uno as she stood in front of him. Uno dick print said all she needed to know. He had been wanting to fuck Ashley for so long that he couldn't hold it back any longer. Standing up Uno took control of things. Undressing down to his boxers and shoes, now it was Ashley's turn to see what she had been missing out on.

"Damn," she thought to herself.

"Bend over," Uno said, stroking his penis. For the next ten minutes, Uno pounced on her from the back, making her cum twice already.

"Boy, if I knew the dick was this good, I would have been letting you hit," Ashley said, standing up and leading Uno to her bedroom for round two.

Chapter 33

Today marks a full month since Uno had his newfound freedom. He was so focused on tryna to learn who was who that he didn't notice four weeks had passed by him. In the midst of things, he made sure to check in on Ms. Long a few times. He even talked to Nasty on her office phone tryna pass time because all Nastgy had to do is hit him on the burnout phone he had. Nasty had a week left and he would be home.

Every day, Uno would get dressed and head over to Nasty's big brother Gee trap spot and just fucked with him but in between time, he watched and listened to everything moving in and out of Gee's spot.

Gee was moving pounds after pounds.

"Damn, Uno! When you get out, nigga?" Lil Jay, Ashley's ill brother asked when he walked into the trap and noticed Uno sitting at the table.

"Nigga, look at you! You look good. Let's step out and burn this," Lil Jay suggested holding up a fat blunt.

Uno, Gee and Lil jay passed the blunt back and forth for the next few minutes while chopping it up about the old times when Uno, Lil Jay and Nasty used to beat dudes their age and older up. When the blunt was over, Lil Jay and Uno exchanged numbers and Lil Jay hopped in an Audi A8 and sped off.

"Damn, this bitch is popping!" Uno said to Gee as he went into the trap.

Years ago, my brother's had it popping like this with the dope, now it's weed, he thought as his phone rang.

"Hello?" he picked up

"Hey baby, I miss you so much," Punkin said.

Hearing Punkin's voice on the other line put a smile on his face.

"Aye, I miss you too baby," Uno replied

"I didn't want anything but to hear your voice, so I'm going to let you get back to what you were doing," Punkin said before hanging up.

Uno stood on the porch and cautiously surveyed the block looking for anything suspicious before heading back into the trap.

Gee was moving around the tap sacking up pounds while listening to Young Dro mixtape when Uno entered. The whole table was stacked with money with diff colored bonds on them.

"Damn, all them pounds about to be sold?" Uno asked as he took a sit next to Gee.

"Nigga, you know if your brothers find out you have been in her, they are going to kick your ass," Gee said. "Shit is jumping today! Gee looked over and caught Uno staring off into LALA land.

"Damn, Lil Bro, I know that look!" he said getting up. It's about da time, when the lion is hungry, it eats and I know you one, so get your own sack; nothing but the best and get some of this money.

As soon as Uno left, he called his cousin Baby J and placed an order for a few pounds. Once they finished going over numbers, they agreed to meet the next morning.

Chapter 34

Within a few days, Uno had the whole ten pounds gone he had copped off his cousin and made over $24,000 selling each ounce for $600 apiece. Knowing how Gee's trap was moving, he knew it was going to be easy money. But weed wasn't really profitable if you smoke, plus it didn't give you the rush dope does when you move blocks. He saw Gee in the kitchen a lot whipping dope up, so he was going to see how the dope game was but still move weed. After grabbing Gee $5,000, Uno called Baby J to place another order.

Since Uno hasn't been spending that much time with Punkin, he decided he would surprise her. Headin' over to Punkin's job at her grandparents' restaurant, he stopped and grabbed a bear, chocolate and a few single roses. Punkin was working with a customer when he walked through the door. When she turned around, she saw Uno standing off in the waiting area holding a big white bear, chocolate and a few roses. She made eye contact with him and smiled as her heart melted.

Punkin would always be his heart. Not only did she hold him down his bid but since he had been home, she had been spending her little check buying him clothes, getting her aunt Sherry to rent cars for him and other things. Uno put every dime she spend to the side. Since Punkin wanted to go to college for hair, he would make that happen for her. He just hated she had to work at the restaurant because Man-Man's mom owned the building next to it.

"Awww, this is so sweet!" She said while smelling the roses. "Baby," she said looking at him suspiciously.

"Just go get ready," he said walking back out of the door.

When she walked out, Uno had the car door open for her which made her wink at him.

"Bae, what are you up to?" she asked him when he got into the car.

"Why I gotta be up to something?" Uno smirked as he pulled off. "Naw, that's just for being a beautiful girl," Uno charmed.

"Boy, boo you're crazy as hell," she responded, blushing.

For the next few minutes, they rode while listening to Lil' Chat until they pulled up in front of Punkin's mom's house.

"Listen baby, go throw on something really nice and pack a bag, you are spending some time with me. I will be back soon."

"Okay, let me get out of here," Punkin said cheesing as she hopped out and rushed up to the house.

When he arrived back at his mom's crib, he got down to business getting himself together for the night.

Meanwhile, Punkin was hopping out of the shower applying lotion over her body before spraying Uno's favorite perfume in the air. Next, she threw on a sexy Calvin Klein dress she got from her auntie, putting on a pair of Sarah Flint heels to finish off her look.

By the time Punkin was walking down the stairs, Uno was pulling up in front of the house. Quickly putting lip gloss on her luscious lips, she grabbed her belongings and headed out the door.

"Damn," Uno said, observing how sexy Punkin looked with her hair pinned up showing off her pretty face. He shook his head at the thought of being home a month and a half and only hit it twice but it was more than sex with him. He saw a real future with her.

"You look good and smell even better," Uno complimented as he kissed her. Uno pulled off and headed to their destination. Not long after pulling off, they were pulling up to West-Inn hotel. After valet parking, the two headed inside to check in. Uno had an enchanting night planned.

"Mr. and Mrs. Brandon," Uno told the desk clerk with a big smile. "Also, I would like to have a platter of garlic grilled shrimp sent to my room please," Uno said, handing the desk clerk a wad of cash. You can keep the change," he said walking off.

Since the bus boy took all their bags to the room, Uno decided to kill time and take Punkin on a little walk downtown. The night was beautiful with the star shining bright. Twenty minutes later, the two laughed and giggled as they walked into their room. Their bag sat by the door and the table was set for two, with their food sitting before two candles.

"Baby, this is so sweet," Punkin said crying.

"Stop crying baby and have a sit," Uno said, pulling out her chair so they could eat and talk.

As they enjoyed each other, they romantically feed each other not realizing hours passed by.

Getting up, Punkin immediately stripped out of her dress and walked over to the radio to put on her slow mix. Uno walked over to the bed and laid back like a fat mac.

Uno smiled as Punkin approached the bed wearing nothing. His dick got hard. Punkin looked at him, smiled, and then eased onto the bed.

Bending down she kissed his lips.

"Baby, tonight is your night. I want you to sit back," Uno said.

"Not happening," Punkin said, feeling the wine cooler, she drank. Getting on all fours, she looked at him and said,

"I want you to tear this pussy up tonight."

Getting up, Uno walked behind her and slapped her ass cheeks watching the little ass she had jiggle. She arched her back. Uno grunts.

"Damn … Big, Juicy putty, Ima tear this shit up," You know Ima go hard on you tonight, don't you?" Uno asked, smiling.

"Spread your legs, baby," Uno demanded looking at her little cheeks and pussy from the back.

"Suck this pussy, muthafucka," she said, glancing at him from over her shoulder.

Bending down, he flicks his tongue over her ass hole, then kissed it before dipping it in.

"Baby, I love the way you're making love to this ass," she moaned loudly.

She eyed him over her shoulders, licking her lips.

His hard chiseled body was positioned in the back of her with sweat. His scrumptiously thick seven-inch dick stabs at the center of her pussy, teasingly. He pulls open her ass again, then buried his face in it.

"Yeah, baby eat it up, niggah. Lick this sweet hole. Hmmm hmmm, make love to it with that thick wet tongue.

Two hard smacks sting her ass, causing her pussy to clench.

"Oooh, yes baby … I need to feel you inside me.

Uno stroked his dick in his hand. She coaxed him to put a finger in her ass hole. Jabbing his middle finger inside, he slowly finger-fucked her ass getting it ready for a deep fucking.

Reaching under her, Punkin played with her clit getting herself wetter.

"You ready for this dick?"

"I stay ready, niggah," She said jiggling her ass for him.

He stabs his dick deep inside her ass.

"Hmmm, Yess, that's it. Fuck this ass, niggah. Oooh, yes baby, don't be scared to beat it up."

He started fucking her faster pounding her mercilessly, reaching his hand under her and toyed with her clit. Her moaning. His groaning, thrusting into her again and again.

"Damn, ma … aaaah, shit … goddammit … muther fuck … ass is good," he groaned.

"Beat it up then, niggah … yeah, you got all that dick in this ass, baby. What's my name niggah?" She asked.

He grunts as her hole clenches around his shaft.

"Punkin, ma … aaaah, fuck … daamnn."

His body jerks as he tightly grabs her waist …

"Mmmm … aaah … mmmph …

"Give me that nut niggah … got this ass wide open. Cum all up in this ass, baby … I'm jabbing two fingers upward into my pussy stroking my g-spot. There ya go niggah … fuck this ass … ooh, yes … I'm cumming."

She felt his spasm shoot through her as he pumped harder inside her. A few minutes later, he pulls out her and coated her ass and back.

***

The next morning, Uno dropped Punkin off at home and then headed out to the mall to meet Baby J. He arrived at the mall and parked in the back so he could see the whole parking lot. He placed his gun on his hip, threw the backpack in the trunk, and headed inside where he grabbed a bite to eat from a place called "Dionne's soul Food" that sat in the food court, while he waited on Baby J's call.

Halfway through his meal, he got the call. Baby J explained he was waiting on his connect to come through but knew where he could get the same stuff at the same price. After Baby J gave him a new address, he got up to throw away his trash and headed out.

As Baby J was pulling up to the address as well, Uno pulled behind him and shut the engine off. The front door swung open and they were instructed to come inside. When they walked into the house, they immediately started scanning their surroundings to make sure they were alone.

Keeping his back on the wall and gun in hand, Uno was ready to get down to business.

"I will be out there in a hot second," the voice said from the back.

Uno knew his cousin wouldn't set him up but he didn't know who the dude was and he didn't trust him. Uno removed the backpack and sat it on the floor in front of him. The dude was already prepared. Uno pounds were on the kitchen table stacked up. There was a sofa off in the corner. I know this muthafucka ain't getting shit through the furniture company, Uno thought.

"You got the money?" The voice asked, walking into the room.

Uno picked up the backpack, threw it to him then walked up and grabbed one of the pounds off the table to inspect it.

"Is this the same shit my cuz got?" Uno asked, sniffing the buds.

"What's ya name, You look like someone I know?" Uno asked

"First, yes it's the same as your cuz, and second, my name is Flow?" I have family from around ya way. Uno looked at Baby J who scanned the house because something didn't feel right.

"Yo, Flow, let me use ya restroom," Uno asked.

"Down the hall, it's the first door on the left."

Uno heard down the hallway, snooping. He didn't have to use the restroom, he just wanted to see what else was in the house. Looking into one of the rooms, he saw more boxes. Uno peeped back down the hall and when he saw that Baby J was talking to him, he slipped into the room. Looking inside one of the boxes, he saw club pictures of him with females, some of him, Man-Man and other nigga's. Uno gritted his teeth and nodded his head. Grabbing the duct tape off Flow's dresser, he wrathfully charged into the living room.

"Did you find it?" Flow asked as he continued counting the last stack of money.

"Bruh, what's happening?" Flow stuttered with sweat beads dripping down his face.

"Man fuck all this talking get up!" Uno ordered.

Flow quickly jumped to his feet.

"Now, I want ya to listen. You have two choices. We can do this the hard way or the easy way. The choice is up to you. Now I'ma asked you, where's the shit at?"

"Bruh, come on, don't do this!" Flow pleaded

"Pow!" Baby J popped him in the leg.

"Nigga, if you don't come with the answer, I'ma going to take it that ya want to do this the hard way." Baby J yelled.

"It's in the back!" Flow quickly screamed

"Go check cuz?" Baby J told Uno. Uno came back into the living room holding a small safe.

"It's fifty grand in there!" Flow said. Uno looked at the safe and caught an attitude.

"This all the fuckin money you got?" Uno asked slapping Flow across the face with his pistol.

"That's all of it!" Flow cried as piss trickled down his leg.

"All this stunting your cousin is doing around the city and all ya got is fifty put up? I should kill both of you niggahs. Where the rest of the shit at niggah?"

"It's all in the boxes around the kitchen and living room," Flow replied, holding pressure on his gunshot.

Uno started smiling when he looked into the box on the floor and the box was filled with fifteen pounds in it and the next two had the same.

"Lay your bitch ass down!" Uno ordered duct taping Flow's hands to his feet.

Uno and Baby J quickly moved the boxes to the door and grabbed the pounds off the table into another box. The more he thought about the lick, the happier he became. Uno grabbed all his money back up and stuffed it back into its bag. Looking out the peephole to make sure no one was looking or coming and when Uno saw that it was clear, they saw Flow tryna get loose. Walking over to Flow, Uno popped him in the knee cap and that instantly made him cry out again.

Thought we were out of her, huh?"

Flow looked up in their eyes and saw the boogeyman.

Both Uno and Baby J pointed their gun at Flow and let it spark, lighting his ass up.

After Uno called everyone and told them he was getting a new number, he handed the homeless man that was sitting on the corner of 29th MLK the old phone and $200.

"If you want to get on your feet, that's a come-up. I push weed," Uno said to the homeless man before speeding off.

Uno got back to the crib and put everything up, got fresh and headed back out to celebrate his come-up.

Chapter 35

Punkin sat in the clinic confused about how she let Uno knock her up. She missed her time of the month. She sat in the house all weekend long cleaning and pondering on if she was doing the right thing. Since Uno came home, their relationship bloomed. She starts crying every time she thought about their relationship because she was so in love with Uno.

Punkin nervously wiggle her fingers as she sat in the chilly, eerie room of the clinic. She called her little brother L when she woke up to talk to him but after five minutes, he rushed her off the phone saying he had to do something important and he would see her when he came home.

Every time she tried to talk to Uno about her being pregnant, she got scared of the response she would get. She had all types of things running through her head. They were both 14 years old; too young to be having kids. She knew Uno always told her that he wanted to build a big family with her.

"Punkin Walton?" A young black nurse called out from a window.

Giving a warm smile, Punkin stood up.

"Hi. I'm Walton," she said walking up.

"Follow me please," the nurse said, then led her to a back room.

Punkin slowly walked down the chilly hallway like it was a walk of shame. Her stomach did somersaults and it felt like

155

she could puke up her breakfast at any time. She didn't know if she was pass out or not. Uno told her he had to) leave to do something important and he will see her when he came home.

At this point, Uno was the only one that didn't know. Her mother told her she had to do something because she wasn't taking care of any new baby.

"You can have a seat on the table," the young nurse told Punkin

"Relax, you seem like you're nervous," the nurse said moving about the room.

"How do you know?" Punkin asked with a smile.

"I see the way you keep moving," the nurse said checking Punkin's blood pressure.

Punkin just nodded her head.

"It's going to be ok," the nurse said with a smile on her face. I know this is a hard decision for you to make by yourself, so if you have a pinch of doubt in your mind, you should take the time to think about it," the nurse said.

"Can you excuse me for a hot second while I make a call?"

The nurse just nodded in understanding.

"Thank you," Punkin said, then grabbed her purse and headed outside to place her call.

While standing in front of the clinic, Punkin held her breath waiting on Uno to pick up the phone.

"Hello?" Uno answered in a steep voice with a little attitude.

"Can we talk or is this a bad time?" Punkin asked.

"Naw baby, why would you say that? You can have all my time," Uno said, sitting up in the bed.

"Well, I want you to know that I'm at the clinic and I missed my time of the month but momma told me I couldn't keep the baby and to do something about it, so I thought about getting an abortion.

"What y'all tripping thinking y'all can do that without talking to me first. I want all mine seed, Uno said with attitude. If you do that, I promise you I'm going to kill all y'all," Uno said hanging up the phone in Punkin's ear.

***

Harding was packed as always when Uno pulled up and parked in front of Butler's where a small crowd was gathered outside. They stood around conversing while they smoked cigarettes and weed and drank their drinks. Everyone seemed to enjoy the loud music that could be heard coming from someone's car.

It had only been a week and a half since he and Baby J touched Flow, and he had leased over twenty pounds not counting the last ten he was about to unload on his people.

It was a sunny Wednesday outside. When Uno grabbed his phone, he saw a group of females coming out of Butler's looking at him and that put a smile on his face. Uno headed inside to grab a bite to eat. He hit ones with dap and head noodles with the few hitters that were in the spot. He stood off to the side so he could see the door.

After placing his order, Uno sat down and debated with himself if he should grab his own trap since he didn't need to be in Gee's anymore. He was sitting on a little over a hundred thousand dollars, the most he have ever had in his life. At age 14, Uno was making a name for himself and stepping out of the shadows of his brothers. If Ant knew Uno was moving around, he would be mad whereas on the other hand, Big Dawg would have been happy to see him standing on his own. Too bad Big Dawg had to go to prison for a year.

By nightfall, Uno had handled all his business in the streets so he was headed to pick up Punkin so they could head to the police auction. He was about to cop himself something nice. Even tho it was nightfall, the auction was swarming with hitters trying to find something to pop out with. Uno stood next to Baby J, scooping out the various cars.

"Cuz, do you know what ya looking for?" Baby J leaned over and asked him in his ear.

"I'll know when I see it," Uno replied. Baby J was getting heated as he stood watching car after car pass by.

"There her fine ass go!" Uno said as he walked over and inspected a Land Rover.

Baby J was relieved, then followed behind him. Uno popped the hood and let Baby J check to make sure everything was right so Uno could drive it off the lot. Baby J stepped back, smiled and then threw both of his thumps in the air.

"Get it!" Uno told Baby J. "I'm putting it in momma's name." Baby J walked off to go find his female friend that worked at the auction so he could pay her off.

"I found one baby," Uno told Punkin as she walked up to him and hand him water.

After cashing out, Uno rode off the lot in a new truck with Baby J following him to the paint shop.

The next week, Uno smiled when he pulled up to the paint shop and saw his truck in the front shining. The sunlight beamed down so mercilessly on the paint job making it sparkle. He walked around inspecting it for any flaws and saw none. Everything looked pretty good to him, so he headed inside to pay the clerk the remaining two grand on his balance and to grab his keys.

"So what do you think about your baby out there?" Pone asked him when he walked through the door of the shop.

"You did your thang," Uno told him, handing him his cash.

"Appreciate it," Pone said, handing over the keys.

Uno threw the keys to the rental to CR. "Follow me," he said.

LR was admiring Uno's whip and himself riding down the street in it. He wanted to be like his bro. Uno came home and started doing good for himself. He didn't let boy school make him bitter.

Later that day, Uno filled his truck up and explored the city, getting his shine on. He watched everybody he passed trying to see who was riding in that truck sitting on "22"

Chapter 36

For the past few weeks, Uno has been partying, hanging out and blowing money fast. He was sexing so many women on the reg that he felt he never did a bid in boy school.

Every day that past, Uno found himself in the hottest spot throwing money showing out, and that's what got his name ringing in the streets as the young nigga to see. That's how he bagged the victim who lay next to him. He looked over her body and shook his head at the outline of the fine thick specimen underneath the sheets.

Raven was what you called hood all around from the way she walked, ate, talked and hustled. She stood about 5'5", had a Hershey complexion, gray eyes, a cute shape, and a short bob hairdo. She did any and everything to keep everything she needed. She used her body to trick men into paying her bills. Poverty was all she knew.

"Checkout time is in 30 minutes," Uno said, shaking Raven. She sat up in bed, and looked around while combing her fingers through her hair.

Twenty minutes later, Uno pulled in Sutton Place out post and let Raven out of the car. While out east, Uno decided to stop at Washington Mall to see what new clothes were out. By 12 o'clock, Uno was headed to Punkin's job. It then dawned on him how little time he had been spending with Punkin since getting home from boy school. He had been so caught up dealing with females all over the city and partying that he had been neglecting the one he should've been giving the most attention. What put the icing on the cake was when he realized he hadn't got on from Baby J or hustled in a few weeks. He made a mental note to himself to check his bankroll when he got home.

As Uno headed off the highway, he thought about Punkin and smiled. She was a good female, and he loved her like no other. She had a go-getter mentality like himself and that's one of the reasons he connected with her on another level. She was just a female version of himself and people had been telling him that for a while.

It's crazy that usually when he sexed females, he just went on about his business, but with Punkin, the sex was amazing and then the conversation make it even better because they could joke and have fun.

Punkin was just walking out the front door of the restaurant looking good in a Sequin Rosario outfit with shades to match. Uno had got her some clothes when he went out of town on a weekend. She looked so good and innocent to the point it made Uno feel worst for not spending time.

"I gotta get myself on the right track," he said to himself, getting out to walk around so he could open the car door for Punkin.

After getting in the car, Punkin saw Uno had been to the mall again. She couldn't do anything but roll her eyes at Uno.

"I see you have been to the mall again, huh?" she commented.

"Ye …" Uno stuttered. Punkin rolled her eyes again. "Are you busy tonight again?"

"Naw, we can do whatever you wanna do," Uno said, smiling, thinking everything was good.

Irritated with Uno, Punkin just shook her head. It had been a few weeks since they had been out to do anything. She decided it was time to enlighten Uno.

"You know, ever since you hooked up your car and started moving around, you changed up on me," she looked over into his eyes and said.

"What do you mean by that?" Uno asked lightweight mad. Punkin rolled her eyes. "Everything is all about Uno!" Uno couldn't argue with her," she was right to feel whatever type of way. He had gotten so caught up in the lifestyle that he had been neglecting not only Punkin but his family.

"Listen baby, if I disrespected you in any kind of way, I truly apologize. You know I was in boy school for some time. I've just been enjoying all the stuff I missed out on, feel me? You don't know how it feels to be caged up then let free."

"I can't say I understand but I feel you, but you owe me," Punkin responded with a smile while rubbing her stomach.

"You got that," Uno said as he pulled up in front of her mother's crib.

"Baby, call the movies and find us something late to go see. We'll go grab a bit to eat first and then we'll catch the movie. How does that sound?" he asked while leaning over to kiss her on the cheek.

"I'll call you and let you know what time the movie starts," she said, hopping out smiling.

Uno sat and watched as she entered the house before pulling off and headed to the crib.

The first thing Uno did when he entered the crib was head to his safe. He was in disbelief at the number, so he recounted it again carefully.

"Twenty-thousand?" he said to himself. He was light headed and the room started spinning. He couldn't believe in two months he'd blown over a hundred. He felt silly for killing Flow and not doing shit with the money. Easy comes, easy goes, he thought to himself. He knew he got too caught up in the moment of thoughtless splurging. He knew he had to get back on the grind.

After cussing himself out, Uno hopped in the shower. Punkin called, he and she agreed to dine at Jacqueline's soul food before catching a movie. It was a little past six o'clock and the movie started at ten, so Uno was going to swing by Punkin's crib to pick her up around 7:30 p.m.

While in the shower, Uno had a lot of thoughts running through his mind. He had been out for two in a half months and head-bodied someone for the first time. He could tell that his cuz Baby J did that shit before, he needed to grab his own crib because Punkin was due in a few months and he wanted her to just focus on school and be the best mother, and he was tired of having to use his brother's crib or spending money on hotels to sex females. He knew his mom and lil sister would be mad but he had to spread his wings a little. He will keep his room still.

"Hey, Lil' Fella, let me holla at you for a minute!" Ant yelled for Uno when he came out to the front door. Smiling, Uno swagged over to Ant's car.

"What's up, Big Bro and Cousin Bird?" he said, giving the two dap.

"Have a seat on the car." They waited till Uno sat on the hood in between the two. Then Ant threw his hand on Uno's shoulder and with a sincere look on his face, "Bro, I'm worried about you. I have been hearing a lot of shit and I've been watching shit too. Lately, all I've been seeing is you around here driving around in that truck, with all these new clothes and jewelry. Nigga, your eyes … they don't have the same look they did when you stood before us on the porch."

Uno was all ears. Damn everyone has seen it but me? he thought.

Ant continued. "I'm not going to keep you long, Lil Bro, but I'ma leave you with this; see, I've been where you are! The spending, the women, the partying, and riding around. Money changes people … their presence, their attitudes, and their actions. If you are going to be out here hustling, have a reason to hustle. Don't be out here doing it just to be doing it. Same shit we told Baby J. Y'all went away to boy school for years, use what you learned in there and from seeing me, Big Dawg and Bird and apply it to yourself. You have principles that you live by. If you compromise those principles, then you will lose sight of who you are." Uno sat in deep thought and let Ant's words sink in. "Money comes and goes. You can get it but the hardest part is keeping it," Ant said.

"Listen, Lil Cuz, use your head and you'll go far. Surround yourself with positive and ambitious people, and you'll never go broke. Life is like chess and every move you make can cost you. Always remember a fool act on emotion, but a smart man thinks everything out," Bird said pointing at his temple.

"Trust me, Cuz it works for us. Look at US!" Bird said, smiling, standing up. "Nigga, we've been having money for years and that's because we've invested our money. Big Dawg is gone to prison but still making money. You see, some people hustle for the fame and street cred but when we were standing on the block, it was for you and Baby J, so y'all didn't do this but I guess it's in y'all blood," Bird said.

"Thanks, Big Bro and Cuz, I needed this talk," Uno said, as he embraced one after the other.

Uno saw the time. "I gotta go pick up Punkin. I'll see y'all soon," he said, then walked over and hopped in his truck.

Ant waved at Uno as he sped off. He could've easily made a phone call and erased all of Uno's problems.

Chapter 37

A week had passed since Ant and Bird pulled down on Uno and had a pep talk with him. Ever since that day, Uno had fallen back on spending and got back to what he knew, grinding. Things were moving very slowly for Uno. For some reason, Uno felt like he was grinding for nothing. He needed his hands on a steady connect. His brothers would never serve him saying they are not going to be the reason I get fucked. He was still grinding the weed but lately, he had been copping a few ounces off of different niggahs around the hood to stay afloat.

Uno pulled into the shell gas station on 38th and Capitol to fill up his truck.

It was a bright, sunny, beautiful Saturday, and today, he just wanted to cruise around the city blowing some trees and get his mind right. He was debating with himself on which city he wanted to hit because he was getting tired of the same thing every day.

"Damn, the city done changed a lot," Nasty said, as he waited for the light to turn green. Nasty thought his eyes and mind were playing tricks on him. *Damn, that nigga looks like Uno*, he thought to himself, staring at the truck.

"That *is* my nigga!" Nasty said, making a U-turn.

Meanwhile, numerous girls walked by, waving and flirting with Uno while he pumped his gas. When an unfamiliar H2 Hummer with dark tints pulled up beside him, he instinctively eased his .45 cal off his waist.

Nasty hopped out of the truck and jokingly threw his hands in the air. "Damn, bro, don't shoot!"

"Oh shit, nigga! I thought you still had a few weeks?" Uno asked as the two embraced each other.

"I got out yesterday. Ms. Long got me out. Gotdamn, nigga, you weren't playing no games, were you?" He walked around inspecting Uno's Land Rover.

"I ain't on shit," Uno said like it was nothing. Nasty nodded his head while checking out Uno's wardrobe and his jewelry game. From the outside looking in, Uno was executing his plan.

"So damn, nigga, why didn't you pull up over moms house yesterday?"

Nasty shrugged his shoulders. "I just went by and saw my kids, hit Ashley up for a shot, and then spend the rest of the day getting my mind right. I had a lot to think about.

"I feel you, playboy," Uno said. Truthfully, hearing Ashley's name turned his stomach. In their boy school bid, all Ashley did was fuck Nasty. "I know what you're thinking, bro," Uno gave him a head nod.

"Who whip you driving anyway, Uno nodded his head towards the Hummer truck.

"That's Ashley, sister BD Two-Tall. He is fucking with Man-Man from the hood," Nasty said.

Uno let out a laugh, "You talking about Pooh, Yeah I know that chick, I was with her the other night," Uno said. Anyway, where are you laying your head at?" Uno asked Nasty.

"I'm chilling at Momma's crib." And yeah, my cousin told me you have been creeping around with her since you been home," Nasty laughed.

Uno let out a laugh as well but was hot that Ashley talked his business, so he was going to call and cuss her ass out.

"I got that bread at the crib for you too," Nasty said.

"Coo, you know Punkin's pregnant now. She will be due in a few months.

"What?" Punkin!," Nasty said laughing.

"Bro, we gotta get you out of those prison wear," Uno said, tagging on Nasty's pants.

"Well, follow me back over to the hood to drop dude truck back off," Nasty said, hopping in the hummer.

After dropping off the truck and swinging by the liquor store, Uno leaned back in the passenger seat while Nasty drove downtown to the mall.

As usual on a Saturday, the mall was packed when they pulled into the parking garage. The two sat in the truck puffing on a blunt Uno rolled while passing their bottle. A few minutes later, the two emerged from the car, eyes red with a nice buzz off the bottle.

"Here take this," Uno said, passing Nasty five thousand dollars.

Nasty's face lit up. Not only had Uno split the bread before he left, but he was now giving him money to spend on clothes.

For the next two hours, Uno went from store to store accumulating bag after bag. Nasty and Uno dressed totally different from each other.

Nasty loved nothing but hood shit, whereas Uno was a fly dude who can dress for any occasion. Uno just had this standout presence.

The two were having a ball until they walked into the food court and spotted something that altered their mood.

Man-Man and his entourage mobbed through the entrance of the mall like they owned the world. Man-Man's name was ringing hard in the streets. Ever since Man-Man's cousin left him dope and spots, Man-Man has been getting money.

Man-Man's crew was decked out in the latest fashions from head to toe. Every girl's eyes were on them as their jewelry glistened as they walked through the mall. Uno gritted his teeth when he and Man-Man made eye contact. The two shared a personal beef.

"What's up, Uno and Nasty? Y'all need to get y'all weight up because that little spending y'all just spent is what we throw in parties," Man-Man said with a sarcastic smirk on his face when he walked by.

Man-Man's crew sized Uno and Nasty up and then smiled as they walked off. Nasty held Uno back from getting at Man-Man.

"Chill out, bro! Fuck them niggas! We gonna get our time!" Nasty said as they watched Man-Man and his crew mob through the mall deep.

"Let's get up outta here," Uno said as they both stormed towards the entrance.

Uno's mind seemed distant as he headed into the city.

"You know I really appreciate the love bruh," Nasty said over the Yung Joc CD.

Uno snapped out of his daze. "We family, nigga! That's how family supposed to take care of themselves. Ant got something for you too."

The two rode in silence for a moment before Nasty broke the silence.

"Lil Bro, I gotta get my hustle on," Nasty said, taking a sip from the bottle. You know how a nigga feels when the money ain't right. Shit, bro. I'm thinking about hollering at this one nigga Hip-Hop Ashley fucks with to see if he would hit me off. Shit, I thought about getting at his ass," Nasty said.

The two laughed.

"Who the nigga fucks with anyways," Uno asked.

"I think them nigga's Man-Man," Nasty said eyeing Uno.

With an idea popping in his mind, Uno rubbed his chin and said, "I wonder if the nigga got some weight?"

"Call Ashley and tell her you tryna holla at him!" Uno told him, as he took a few pulls from the blunt and exhaled a cloud of smoke.

"What you tryna cop bro?" Nasty asked when Uno handed him over his phone.

"Shit, I want to cop two bricks," Uno lied. "But I'll cop a few ounces off him first to see if it do what it supposed to do. Then if it's A-1, I'll get back with him on the up and up.

After Ashley asked a hundred and one questions on how he got so much money so fast and he was now getting home, Ashley ended up hooking up a meeting between Hip-Hop and Nasty for seven o'clock.

Later that night, the two met up with Hip-Hop and copped a few ounces off him. Uno gave Ashley a few hundred dollars for making the transaction at her parents' crib and went to drop the work off at his mom's crib. Then he and Nasty went out searching for some new pussy. Within the hour, they were headed to a hotel with two fine-ass females.

***

Punkin promptly arrived at Uno's mom's spot at 9:30 a.m. with the rental car he had requested. She stood on the porch as she rang the doorbell.

"I'm coming!" Uno yelled, hopping out of the shower wet. Punkin folded her arms, sucked her teeth, and pouted when he opened the front door.

"I thought you were gonna be ready to go?"

"Just give me one minute!" he said, kissing her before leaving her standing in the living room while he went back into the bathroom.

Punkin sat down on the loveseat. While she waited on Uno, she gazed over at all the family pictures in the entertainment center, which she always did when she was over at the house. Uno's little sister and cousin Baby J resembled Ant so much that you would have thought they were brothers and sisters.

"It's time to get your own place!" She yelled to Uno.

169

"I'm working on that now!" he yelled from his bedroom door. "Why are you so worried about me getting my own crib?" he asked when he walked into the living room.

"Cause I would like to get my fuck on at your place and not here, your sisters or a hotel," Punkin said.

Uno smiled. "I'll tell you what then. Since you are so in a hurry for me to break your back in, in my own spot, that's your little assignment. Find me a place."

"Fine then," Punkin said, grabbing her purse as they both headed for the front door.

Uno hopped in his truck, and Punkin followed him out to a storage unit on the south side. Realizing how silly it was to blow through all that money in a few months, Uno had Punkin's auntie rent a storage unit to put his truck up for the time being. He was staying two steps ahead and knowing he was about to get to the money, he didn't want his truck to be hot.

After parking his truck in the unit and locking it up, he hopped in with Punkin.

Dropping Punkin off at her cousin's crib, LR ran out of the house and jumped into the car and the two headed to the hood to get on the ring. As he cruised through the hood, he just shook his head at how much have changed. The hood had flipped over and all kinds of new faces were hugging the block. It wasn't full of life like when Ant, Bird and Big Dawg were standing out here. Although a little money still rolled around the hood, most of the money went to Hip-Hop. Word on the street was that Man-Man was supplying Hip-Hop with rocks so big that niggas couldn't compete. The only clientele who remained loyal to the ones in the head are the ones who have been staying over there for years, but even some of them went and copped from Hip-Hop.

Uno was on a mission to get it rocking. He didn't care what the next nigga was doing because he was too focused on himself. He had been taught by the best, and it was time to put his skills to work.

That entire day, Uno and LR made their rounds, giving everybody testers so word could spread that they were back in the hood. As he posted up on Udell, he stared at the house they use to stay in back in the day. He thought about when they had a Shrimp Hut on the corner and he reminisced on all the good times he, Nasty and a few others shared. It felt good to be in the hood. He smiled as the whole scenery brought back so many vivid memories. He took a swing out of the bottle and puffed on the blunt he was blowing as he and LR walked down Udell.

Uno felt a funny feeling wash over his body as a cool breeze came through and ruffled his shirt. He smiled and look down at the chain and ring he got from Big Dawg. He glanced up at the sky and said a silent prayer.

By nightfall, Uno and LR had made over five thousand and felt content with their first day out there.

"Big Bro, I'm trying, got be out here with you every day," LR said counting the money Uno gave him.

Utilizing everything he had learned from Ant, Big Dawg, Bird and the streets, it didn't take long for Uno to build up his clientele. In a few weeks, Uno and LR had Udell jumping like the old days. Money was coming in from all angles. Traffic flowed through the hood like it was a detour route.

Uno fulfilled Punkin's wish by pulling up in a truck and telling her it was time to move. He had found himself an apartment on High School Road out west. Thanks to the crackheads from the hood he was able to furnish his entire apartment and still cop a few bricks.

With things looking up for Uno, and with Punkin's birthday, only a few days away, he had a few tricks he was putting together.

Chapter 38

A few days later, Uno had to get up at the crack of dawn to prepare for Punkin's birthday. Although she wasn't due to arrive home until later in the day, he still wanted to make sure everything was perfect for her day. It was rarely you find someone as special as Punkin.

Uno's first stop that morning was to Tiffany's jewelry store, where he picked up a karat solitaire diamond ring he had custom-made, along with a three-karat tennis bracelet. Victoria's Secret was the next stop. There, he purchased a few lingerie sets, along with a few bottles of body wash. He smiled to himself as he watched the cashier gift wrap everything he gotta, excited by the thought of Punkin stripping out of one of the lingerie sets for him.

Uno left the mall and headed straight to Build A Bear where he purchased roses, rose petals, one human-size bear and several different color balloon bouquets. To add to the decor, he even purchased blue silk sheets.

The minute Uno arrived at their crib, he immediately went to work decorating. He started first in the bedroom by changing the room around, then switching his sheets with the silk ones he purchased.

Next, he sprinkled rose petals all over the bed and throughout the room all the way into the hallway. He made sure he made the rose petals leading from the front door to the bubble bath he was going to have waiting. After he finished, he nodded his head in admiration and then checked his Rolex. It was a little past 5 p.m., and Punkin was getting off work, so that gave Uno over an hour before she arrived.

Uno headed into the kitchen, washed his hands, and immediately slapped the pork chops on the counter into its batter, then threw it in the oven. Just like everyone else in his family, he was a master at cooking. He already had the sauce for the chops ready along with the whole potatoes, mac cheese, and a nice salad.

Once dinner was completed, Uno set the table, lit a couple of candles, and then sat the salad and bottle of chilled champagne in the middle of the table. He covered the food up and rushed to hop in the shower.

While Uno showered, he smiled at himself. He couldn't wait to see the look on Punkin's face when she walked through the door.

I'm the truth, he thought to himself. After slipping on a pair of silk Polo pajamas, Uno squirted on a little Polo Blue and surveyed the room.

Lighting the candles around the house to give it that smell mixed with the food, he then put the bracelet on the bear's arms and sat the ring on the lap.

Meanwhile, Punkin was climbing up the stairs and sniffing the air.

"Damn, somebody's throwing down," she said. The more she climbed, the stronger the aroma got. Punkin smiled when she made it to the top and realized the aroma was coming from their apartment.

"This nigga thinks he the truth," She said out of breath.

"Damn, it smells good out here," the couple said who stayed next door to them.

"Thank you and hello, I'm Punkin, we moved in next door," Punkin said.

"I'm Martha and this is my husband Shawn," Martha said, reaching out to shake Punkin's hand.

"When are y'all due and do you know what y'all having," Shawn asked.

"We'll be having a girl and I'm due in a few months," Punkin responded while rubbing her stomach.

Uno heard Punkin's voice talking, so he inspected the house one last time, smiled, and then headed to the front door. He stood waiting for Punkin to knock because she never took her keys. She knocked extra hard.

"Who is this at my door?" Uno asked jokingly.

"Boy, you better stop playing and open this damn door!" Punkin yelled.

"Alright, damn, but take them shoes off," Uno demand. Punkin knew not to play with Uno, so she pouted while taking off her shoes. When Uno finally moved out of the way, she threw her hands over her mouth and said, "Oh my God! Who did this?"

"Go ahead baby! Walk on them," Uno said, as he stepped to the side to let Punkin step on the rose petals.

Once she stepped inside, he directed her towards the beautiful candlelit dinner table. "After you, sexy," he said.

"You are the truth," Punkin said, as Uno pulled out her chair for her to sit.

Punkin sat back and stared in admiration while Uno moved throughout the kitchen heating up dinner and began preparing their plates.

"Here you are" Uno said, placing her plate in front of her.

"Wow! Mmmm, these are good," she said after taking a bite of her chops.

Uno popped the cork on the bottle of Don P, poured himself a glass and poured her some water.

"I'd like to propose a toast."

Punkin smiled and lifted her glass.

"To your 15th birthday," he said and the two clanked their glass.

For the next hour, they giggled and talked while Uno romantically fed Punkin.

"Mmm, that was good," she said.

After cleaning up their mess, Uno reached out his hand for Punkin.

"Come with me," he said, then led her down the hallway to his bedroom. It looked like they were headed down the altar.

When Punkin walked through the bedroom door, all she could do was smile upon seeing the bubble bath with a single white rose and lace lingerie set sitting on top of the counter next to a big puffy towel.

"Baby, I want you to relax, because today is your day," he said while helping her undress. He then helped her into the bath.

"Ahhh, Mmm," Punkin said as she immersed her body into the water.

Uno grabbed the sponge, kneeled before her, and started bathing Punkin. He couldn't resist sucking and licking her neck.

"Goddamn, baby, that feels so good," She moaned. "Can't you wait until we get into the bedroom?" she asked, rubbing his back.

Uno smiled. "Okay baby, but this is to be continued," he replied while grabbing the wash rag and beginning to wash her up.

After washing her, he helped her stand while he grabbed the towel and sat it near.

"Go ahead and finish," he said, patting her on the butt.

"He's crazy," she said to herself, smiling as she finished washing her ass and pussy, then dried off and slipped into the lingerie set. She looked at herself in the mirror.

There was a trail of rose petals leading to the bedroom when Punkin came out of the bathroom. She smiled as she slowly followed them. She couldn't believe her eyes when she entered the bedroom. Staring in amazement, she placed her hand on her chest. She felt so good at that moment that tears poured down her cheeks. She looked at Uno stretched out across the bed in his silk boxers.

He motioned for her with his finger. "All this is for you, baby," he said smiling. "Here is our third wheel," he said, handing out the bear.

Punkin smiled as she cheerfully saw the Tiffany bracelet around the arm of the bear.

"Keep looking baby," Uno said. When Punkin saw the ring hanging off the tennis bracelet, she damn near lost it.

"Oh my God!"

Uno had touched her so deeply that she felt like she had gone to heaven.

Punkin jumped out of her underwear, eased in the bed and started smothering Uno with kisses. "I love you, baby!"

Laying Punkin down, Uno eased on top of her.

"It's your night. I'm the one that supposed to be kissing all over your body," he said with a laugh before he started planting soft kisses all over her.

Hopping up fast scared Punkin as she watched Uno walk over to the flowers that sat on the dresser and took a single rose. Turning the CD player on, Keith Sweat came blasting through the speakers.

Uno was already disappearing under the sheets and started skillfully licking up her body while tailing it with the rose. Punkin moaned and squirmed as she rubbed the back of his head. Uno licked around her navel, then worked his way up to her breast and kissed both of them equally. With her being pregnant her nipples swelled. Uno came up from under the sheet.

"Awww, baby, you're the best," Punkin took the rose and said while smelling it.

Uno didn't respond as he slowly descended his way down to her love box. Her eyes got big as apples when he started massaging her clit with his tongue.

"Oh shit, baby!" She cried out with her mouth open as his fingers went to work going in and out of her pussy. She almost lost it when Uno applied pressure to a magical spot inside her pussy walls. Feeling like she had to piss, Punkin started to push him off so she could get up but Uno grabbed her legs and locked them around his head as he sucked hard.

"Baby, oh shit, I feel I have to piss," Punkin said, not able to hold it back.

Punkin stared dawn at Uno's face and the puddle beneath them.

"I'm just getting started," Uno said, taking out his fingers and sucking her juice off them.

"Mmmm ... damn baby, you taste good," he said, staring into her eyes.

Punkin was in a daze. Uno was really turning her on by licking her juice off his fingers. She didn't know what had just happened to her because she have never experienced it.

Punkin flinched as Uno ran his tongue up her clit, parting her lips with his tongue. Moving his tongue around her clit had every hair on her body at attention. Uno's lick/suck combinations had Punkin feeling like she was on cloud nine. Her body went into convulsions when she looked down at him and watched him slowly slid her pussy lips with his mouth. Two orgasms later, Uno came up with pussy juice all over his face again.

"You ready for the real thing?" he asked. Punkin lay in bed in a daze, trying to catch her breath.

"Oh my God!" she said for the fourth time, gasping for air. Her body just kept shaking.

Uno slowly kissed her neck while he eased inside her.

Punkin flinched a little. "Uno, slow!"

He kissed her on the forehead and then eased a little more of himself inside her.

"Ummm," Punkin moaned in his ear.

Thanks for the foreplay, she was extremely wet. The more Uno eased inside her, the harder she started to breathe. The more he filled her walls up, the more her juices overflowed out of her pussy onto the bed. Before long, Punkin was matching Uno's pace.

"Who's pussy is this," Uno asked, performing slow, deep hard strokes.

Punkin moaned in ecstasy.

"Let me know it's mine," Uno said, digging deeper and stroking fast.

Punkin bites his chest. "Oh, shit, baby … it's yours … it's yours!" she moaned loudly. The more they sexed, the hotter it got in the room. Both bodies had rose petals stuck to them.

He pumped and pumped as he felt the tingling he knew too well. Releasing his hot sperm inside her, Uno's head spun.

The two came together in unison. They squeezed each other tightly.

Punkin's body couldn't stop shaking as Uno lay on top of her with his dick still inside of her cavity.

"That was amazing," Uno whispered in her ear as he rolled off her.

For the next few minutes, she rested her head on Uno's chest listening to his heartbeat, while engaging in a conversion. He was a good listener giving her his undivided attention.

After letting Punkin talk, Uno took her into his arms.

"Time to go again," he said.

By the end of the night, the two had worked their way around the apartment and then ended the memorable night falling asleep on top of roses and in each other's arms. The next morning, Uno handed Punkin a .22

Chapter 39

When Uno and LR pulled up in the good crackhead, Holla-Holla ambushed the car.

"Damn, baby, where y'all been? You've been missing out on money like crazy," Holla-Holla stressed with a couple of bills in her hand.

"I had to drop my BM off at work," Uno said, grabbing his pistol and hopping out of the car.

"Come on boy," Holla-Holla said as she made her way towards her house. After serving Holla-Holla, Uno stepped out on the block and made some rounds. Cutting through the park and messing with some of the kids that were playing, he then handed out dollar bills.

"Thank you, you just like Ant and them!" some of the kids chanted when Uno walked off.

That entire day, Money poured in from all angles. From the time Uno pulled up in the hood, his phone rang nonstop.

"Damn, shit is popping today, Brig Bro!" LR said while going to grab another one out of their spot.

It had been less than two hours since Uno and LR came out of the house and were already sitting on five thousand.

The whole time Uno was grinding, he couldn't stop thinking about the night he had with Punkin. He knew Punkin wanted a commitment but with him, just now coming home and being young was scaring him because he never knew what commitment meant. He knew Punkin was worth being with for the rest of his life.

By three o'clock that evening, they were down to a few grams, and judging by the way the hood was jumping, they knew they will be out of dope soon. It made Uno shitty when he called Hip-Hop to find out he was waiting to re-up.

"I can't believe this shit, Friday and it's jumping like this and I run out of dope," Uno said after hanging up the phone with Hip-Hop.

Just then, both his and LR's phones went off with texts, and after looking down at their phones, they both smiled. It was their people from out south asking to spend. Before they headed out south, Uno swung by Holla-Holla's crib and left her a few rocks to hold her for the night. Uno called Nasty to ask if he wanted to hold the rental because he wants to bring out his truck for the night.

After serving their southside clientele, Uno and LR made a few stops before riding out to Nasty's mom to scoop him.

When Uno pulled up, Nasty was on the porch with a bottle in his hand. Seeing Uno come down the street, Nasty locked up his mom's house and hopped into the ride. As soon as Nasty sat down in the car, Uno threw him a bag of weed and a couple of blunts for him to roll up. LR doesn't smoke, so he knew not how to roll.

As they traveled around the city, the three talked and brought each other up to speed on their lives.

By the time they finished the two blunts, they were arriving at the storage unit. Uno hopped inside his truck followed by LR and inhaled the car air freshener. After backing out and locking up the storage unit, he hit his horn at Nasty, turned up 2Pac, and headed toward his apartment.

The minute they entered Uno's apartment, he began to strip out of his clothes because he was desperately in need of a hot shower.

As he headed to the bathroom, LR headed to the kitchen to grab something to eat.

When the hot water hit Uno's body the tension escaped from it. He stayed in the shower until the water turned cold then he hopped out and dried off.

Walking into his bedroom, his cell phone sounded off back to back letting him know he had waiting texts. He looked at the number.

"Who the fuck … 765-268-2181 #1000?"

His phone sounded off again. This time the display read 765-268-2181 #911. He knew by the 765 that the caller was from one of the surrounding cities. What really caught his attention was the 1000 behind the number, which meant someone was trying to spend $1,000 with him.

"Let me find out who the fuck this is," he said dialing the number on his cell phone.

"Hello?"

"Who the fuck is dis?" Uno asked

"What's up? This is Dawn, can you hook me?" Uno looked at his phone at the time. Damn! He and Punkin were catching the 9:30 pm movie, and it was going on at 8:30 pm, now. He knew it would be hard to make the run and get back in time. He resonated with himself that he could hit the hallway and make it back in time. Besides, a thousand-dollar sale wasn't something you just miss.

"Fuck! Damn!" Uno cursed, remembering that Nasty had the rental or the night.

"So what's up, are you coming?" Dawn impatiently asked. Uno rubbed his head while pacing the floor. He had to contemplate for a minute, then asked, "Where you at?"

"I'm in Anderson on Main Street."

"Damn. Alright. I'll be there in thirty minutes," he said.

"Okay, I'll see you then, baby," Dawn said, then hung up the phone.

Uno grabbed the little stash he had left and counted the rocks he had in the bag. All he had left was twenty-five nice size dubs.

"I know what I'ma do," Uno said to himself, then immediately started breaking down the twenty-five, when he finished he had fifty nice size rocks.

"Thousand dollars, yeah she goes for this," he said as he held the rock up in the air.

Uno grabbed his keys, cell and a few blunts.

"I will be back lil bro," Uno said to LR as he bounced out the door.

Damn, I'ma gonna stick out in this truck," he said while hopping in.

***

When Uno turned down Main Street, he immediately spotted Dawn standing in front of the house. He pulled into a parking spot, looked at her, nodded his head, parked and then walked over to her. He surveyed the block before making a bee-line towards her.

"Hey, boo," Dawn said, then anxiously hand him ten crops hundred-dollar bills.

A suspicious-looking dude standing off to the side made Uno hesitant in handing her the rocks.

"Who the fuck is that dude?" he asked

"Oh … he's just one of my tricks," Dawn replied

"I told you when you were in the city that I wasn't trying to meet no new faces," Uno said.

He cautiously looked around the area before grabbing the bag of rocks out and handing them to her.

"Can I call you later on?" Dawn asked as Uno walked back towards his truck.

"Yeah, next time be by yourself," he replied, then hopped into the truck.

Dawn waved. "By Uno! See you later, sweetie. Uno pulled out into the road and blended into traffic while nervously surveying the area erecting to see police cars popping out.

Uno let out a sigh of relief and smiled when he saw the road was free of police. When Uno pulled up to a stop light, he glanced in his rearview mirror and noticed a police car behind him with the officer on his walkie-talkie. He eased off when the light turned green. He only made it a block away before the officer hit his lights. All Uno could do was shake his head.

"License and registration please, sir," The officer asked when he walked up.

As Uno handed over the requested information, he noticed an unmarked car pulling up.

"I'll be right back, sir," the officer said, walking off towards his police cruiser.

"I can't believe this bull," Uno said. Looking through his rearview, Uno tried to read the officer's body language as he walked back towards the car.

"Is everything ok, officer?" Uno asked with a smile on his face

"Sir, I'm gonna have to ask you to step out of the car."

"For what?" Uno asked.

"Sir, again could you please just step out of the car?" the officer asked, taking a step back with his hand on his gun.

"This is some bullshit," Uno mumbled as he exited his car.

"What the hell's going on," Uno asked when he noticed the tow trucks pulling up behind them.

"Can you please walk to the back of the truck," the officer said.

Doing as the officer instructed, Uno shook his head as he walked around towards the back.

"I'm gonna need you to place your hands on the truck and spread your legs for me.

Glad I left my 9mm at the crib tonight, Uno thought while getting shaken down.

"This is quite a bit of money you have here, sir. Where do you work?" the officer asked as he sat the pile of money on the roof.

What the fuck is all this? Uno wondered. He couldn't believe he let himself get caught slipping like this. The few thousand he had on him was the money he was going to give to Punkin to put up for them.

"Here we go!" the officer said, holding the ten hundred-dollar bills he just got from Dawn in the air for whoever was sitting in the tinted unmarked car to see.

That's when both doors to the unmarked opened up and two males in plain clothes got out.

"What the fuck is this?" Uno asked.

"Sir, you are under arrest," the officer said, grabbing his cuffs.

"For what?" Uno spun around and asked already knowing

"You're under arrest for dealing and possession of crack," the officer said, spinning him back around and cuffing him.

"How the -?" Uno's sentence was cut short when the officer spun him back around towards the unmarked car.

"Remember me?" the driver asked. Uno couldn't do anything but drop his head. I'ma kill that hoe! It turned out the guy who Dawn said was her trick ended up being an undercover cop.

"We're seizing your mom's truck since your car was used in the commission of a drug transaction. We're also seizing all the money unless you have proof you work for this," the officer said with a smirk on his face.

The officer walked Uno towards his cruiser and placed him in the back seat.

Uno's stomach tightened as he watched his car get towed away.

"Damn, I told myself I will never get locked up again," he thought.

Since Uno was turning 16 in a few months, they booked him in Anderson county jail and held him on a hundred-thousand-dollar bond. Once fingerprinted, he had a free call to make, he phoned Punkin, who went crazy when she picked up the phone. After he calmed her down, Uno drilled her everything he needed her to do.

Punkin immediately asked to borrow her mother's car and shot out the door, and started making the rounds and gathering all she needed to get Uno's bond paid.

As Punkin put things together, Uno paced the cage he was in. Since it was night, he knew he wouldn't be bonded out until the wee hours. He sat down and rested his head against the wall. He couldn't believe he was once sitting in the same place he promised himself he wouldn't go again.

That entire night, he couldn't do anything but think about the steps he made to land him back here. He knew he should have listened to his instincts, but greed had gotta the better of him.

"Fuck!" Uno yelled, jumping off the bench.

Ten thousand gone, his truck gone, and not to mention, he had a legal situation. Not only that, he still had to pay his bond and get a lawyer.

"As of today, I swear by any means I'ma going to make any move, I make a big one!" he said. This is the last time I'ma let them put cuffs on me again because I will hold court in the streets next time," he thought to himself as he went to lie down on the bench when he dozed off.

***

The next morning, Uno was awakened by the officer sliding open the cell door.

"Brandon, you're free!' the officer said.

Uno sat up, stretched out, and wiped the sleep out of his eyes. After being processed for release, he walked out of the building to Punkin's mom's car. He got teary-eyed when he saw Punkin balled up in the drive side with her coat over her face.

"You have a good woman on your hands. She's been waiting here since last night," the officer that let him outside.

Uno knocked on the car window waking Punkin up. Punkin smiled when she saw Uno standing there. Opening the door, she jumped into his arms. Uno smiled back and kissed her on the forehead.

"Oh, baby, you had me so scared." Uno let a small laugh out. "Don't worry. I'ma be alright," he said, then threw his arm around her for a big hug.

The minute Uno entered their apartment, he started making calls trying to search for a good lawyer. After he was done, he had a number for Hennessy, an aggressive lawyer known for beating cases. Uno talked with Hennessy reception and scheduled an appointment, then headed to the bathroom to freshen up. Uno knew he was going to be spending a nice piece of change when he pulled up to Hennessy's office and saw her Ferrari parked out front.

When Uno walked through the front door, he thought he was walking into a five-star hotel, so he had to double-check he was in the right building. After making sure he was in the right spot, he made his way up to the secretary's desk.

"Hello, my name is Brandon, I called a while ago to make a two o'clock appointment," Uno said.

The secretary picked up the phone, said a few words and hung up.

"Have a seat sir," she said eyeing Uno.

A mixed female came out of an office in her expensive, custom-made designer pants suit and shook Uno's, Punkin's and her aunt's hands.

During the introduction, Uno's eyes were looking over the woman's expensive timepiece and diamond necklaces. Her white teeth contributed to the effectiveness of her smile. He knew them whites cost a pretty penny.

Hennessy led the group into her office, where she sat down in an extremely plush chair. Uno scanned around

Hennessy's decorated office. She had pictures with actors, athletes, politicians and family members.

"Ummm hmmm. Uhhh. Damn. Ahhh," was all Hennessy said while looking over the case. After looking over the file, all Hennessy could do was shake her head.

"Sir, we have good/bad news, which one do you like to hear first?' Hennessy asked.

"Shit, gimme the bad," Uno said.

"The bad news is that a CI and undercover cop was present when the transaction was made and knowing the prosecutors on your case will try to send ya to prison even though this is your first time. You're facing 40 years and with the witnesses, the case is even more strong."

"Damn," Uno replied, dropping his head.

"Well, what's the good," Uno asked, picking up his head.

"The good news is I see some strong points I can argue."

Uno smiled. That was good music to his ears.

"Can I speak with him alone please?" Hennessy asked Punkin and her auntie.

Punkin looked at Uno for the okay, who nodded his head, and they excused themselves from the office.

After they left the office, Hennessy leaned forward and whispered, "No witness, no case." Then she calmly sat back in her chair.

Uno looked at Hennessy, who had a stern look on her face. He nodded his head in understanding at Hennessy's point.

"How much does a case like this cost?"

"For a case like this, you're looking to drop between ten and fifteen thousand," Hennessy said.

Uno rubbed his head. "You got a payment plan?"

Hennessy leaned forward again. "How much do you have right now?"

'I'ma be honest with you. With them taking my car, my money and me making a bond, all I have to my name is a few thousand right now. But if you give me a few weeks, I can have the whole thing for you."

Hennessy looked down at her calendar on her desk.

"Can you have the rest by New Year's? That way, it gives you a few more months to get yourself together.

"I sure can," Uno said, nodding his head. "Okay, I'll take your case. Did you bring that few thousand with you today?" Hennessy asked with a raised eyebrow.

Uno smiled. "Yeah, I got it." Hennessy cheerfully came from behind her desk, shook Uno's hand and patted him on the back.

"Don't worry yourself. You're just hired the best lawyer in the city!" She said with a smile. "I'm giving you till New Year's because I have a trial coming up in a few weeks that I have to prepare for. You might know Baby J?" She comments to see if he did.

"Yeah, that's my cousin," Uno replied with a smile, then exited the office and stopped by the secretary's desk to pay that few thousand.

As he drove home, he had all types of thoughts running through his head. He was sad because he knew his car and money he grinds so hard for were gone. Plus he didn't know his cousin was fighting a case.

"You gonna be alright, baby," Punkin said as he looked over and saw the stress on Uno's face.

***

Uno felt better after Punkin helped him release all of the tension he had built up inside him. Lovemaking always seemed to temporarily get people's minds off their problems. He felt like he was always on cloud nine when he was inside Punkin.

He looked down at her sleeping peacefully on his chest. She was an angel.

"I love you baby," he said, kissing her face. He had hit the bottom, he thought as he stared up at his ceiling. Although he was at the bottom, at least he was still free to do as is. His birthday and Christmas were around the corner, so he had to pick himself up and come up with a plan because bills were coming in and he still had to pay Hennessy her money. Looking at his gun, he knew what he had to do. After coming up with a plan, he kissed Punkin on the forehead, hugged her tight, and called it a night.

Chapter 40

For the past few months, Uno couldn't catch a break to save his life. It seemed like he was catching pure hell since getting hit with the case. After he pawned everything he owned, he walked away with less than ten thousand and that was only half of what he paid. Punkin had offered to give him her savings and to pawn her jewelry, but there was no way he could let her do that. He was grinding good but every time he turned around, something always came up.

The year was officially out the door. Things weren't going how Uno planned them out to be. His Christmas had been horrible since he couldn't really get his family anything. His New Year's was terrible, his birthday was even more horrible, and then Valentine's Day came around and it tore him up that he had to get a booster to grab something for Punkin. The only light his life had was that a few days after Valentine's Day, Punkin pushed out his first child.

That was last month. Today was March 1st, and Uno was gonna make this month better than his last ones. The hood got so hot, Nasty and LR fucked up a few ounces, his clientele out South had moved out of town to get clean, and his plug was in the county.

It took Uno months to track down Dawn. Being a crackhead she bounced from palace to place but his nigga Lil Rube from Anderson saw her and been keeping eyes on her, so tonight, she was residing at H & K hotel.

Dressed in all black, Uno and Baby J blended in the dark alley watching all activity going on inside Dawn's hotel room. Things couldn't have been more perfect for them. The undercover cop and Dawn were the reason both Uno and Baby J were fighting for their lives. They have been going around the city setting people up.

They sat back and watched through Dawn's hotel window. The two were so gone that they never realized that the party was for all to see.

Baby J and Uno watched them take turns feeding their nose with cocaine. Uno surveyed the area, while Baby J kept an eye on the sleazy hotel.

Dawn's room was in the back of the lot on the first floor.

Baby J and Uno looked at each other while thinking the same thing. These were the only two people who can get them off the streets, so no matter what, they had to be dealt with and that night was the night. Staying close to the wall, they threw on their masks. The closer they got to Dawn's room, the louder the music became. The music really worked in their favor. They looked around one last time when they got to Dawn's room door before peeking inside her room. Dawn and the undercover cop hit more lines while sitting at the table. Looking through the window one last time to see where the two Were, giving Baby J a head nod, he kicked in the door. The music was so loud that they never heard anything or saw the two masked men storm inside.

The undercover cop had his nose on the table when the two came in but once he looked up, Uno dumped two shells inside his head. Blood dripped out of both holes as he fell back, collapsing on the floor.

"The dope and money are in the top dresser!" Dawn cried.

"This is much more than a robbery," Baby J stated, removing his mask.

Dawn almost passed out when she saw Baby J's and Uno's faces.

They both smirked. "You weren't expecting to see our face until you got on the stand," Uno asked. "I swear they made me do it! They have been having us set people up," she said.

Baby J grabbed Dawn by the throat and slid his knife across her neck as her eyes popped out.

"Now it's your turn to sleep," Baby J said in her ear as he let her body hit the floor.

With the key witnesses dead, Uno and Baby J knew they were free men. Throwing their hoodies on, they both eased out of the hotel undetected.

"Be easy Lil Cuz," Baby J said going his way.

"Love Cuz and you do the same," Uno said disappearing into the dark.

Being cautious not to be seen, Uno slipped back into his apartment where he found Punkin still sleeping with Pooder on her chest. He grabbed the baby and put her inside her baby bed then eased himself in the bed beside Punkin. Punkin is going to be my alibi, he thought to himself as he fell asleep cuddling with Punkin.

TO BE CONTINUED...

Lock Down Publications and Ca$h Presents
Assisted Publishing Packages

Due to an increase in the price of services we have increased our prices. The prices below reflect the price increase as of 11/1/24.

BASIC PACKAGE $699 Editing Cover Design Formatting	UPGRADED PACKAGE $1000 Typing Editing Cover Design Formatting Upload eBooks to Amazon Upload Paperback to Amazon
ADVANCE PACKAGE $1,400 Typing Editing (line editing/content) Cover Design Formatting Copyright Registration Proofreading Upload eBooks to Amazon Upload Paperback to Amazon	LDP SUPREME PACKAGE $1,700 Typing Editing (line editing/content) Cover Design Formatting Copyright Registration Proofreading Set up Amazon Account Upload eBooks to Amazon Upload Paperback to Amazon Advertise on LDP's Amazon and Facebook Page

***

Other services available upon request.
Additional charges may apply

Lock Down Publications
P.O. Box 944
Stockbridge, GA 30281-9998
Phone: 470 303-9761
Email: lockdownpublications@gmail.com

Submission Guideline

Submit the first three chapters of your completed manuscript to ldpsubmissions@gmail.com. In the subject line add **Your Book's Title**. The manuscript must be in a Word Doc file and sent as an attachment. Document should be in Times New Roman, double spaced, and in size 12 font. Also, provide your synopsis and full contact information. If sending multiple submissions, they must each be in a separate email.

Have a story but no way to send it electronically? You can still submit to LDP/Ca$h Presents. Send in the first three chapters, written or typed, of your completed manuscript to:

LDP: Submissions Dept
P.O. Box 944
Stockbridge, GA 30281-9998

DO NOT send original manuscript. Must be a duplicate. Provide your synopsis and a cover letter containing your full contact information.

Thanks for considering LDP and Ca$h Presents.

NEW RELEASES

BLOODLINE OF A SAVAGE 1-3
THESE VICIOUS STREETS 1-3
RELENTLESS GOON 1-3
BY PRINCE A. TAUHID

THE BUTTERFLY MAFIA 1-3
BY FUMIYA PAYNE

A THUG'S STREET PRINCESS 1&2
BY MEESHA

CITY OF SMOKE 3
BY MOLOTTI

GET IT IN SLUGS 1 &2
BY B. STALL

STANDING ON HER BUSINESS 1&2
BY DG SANTANA

STEPPERS 1,2&3
THE REAL BADDIES OF CHI-RAQ
BY KING RIO

THE LANE 1&2
BY KEN-KEN SPENCE

THUG OF SPADES 1&2
LOVE IN THE TRENCHES 2
CORNER BOYS
BY COREY ROBINSON

TIL DEATH 3
BY ARYANNA

THE BIRTH OF A GANGSTER 4
BY DELMONT PLAYER

PRODUCT OF THE STREETS 1-3
BY DEMOND "MONEY" ANDERSON

NO TIME FOR ERROR
BY KEESE

MONEY HUNGRY DEMONS 1-2
BY TRANAY ADAMS

HUB CITY MENACE 1-3
BY J. WHITE

A THUGGISH PASSION 1&2
LAND OF DA HOOLIGANZ 1-4
KILLAZ ON STANDBY 1&2
BY IRA B.

FO'EVA ROLLIN 1&2
BY ASSA RAYMOND BAKER

THE LEVEL UP 1&3
BY LUXURY KING

Coming Soon from Lock Down Publications/Ca$h Presents

IF YOU CROSS ME ONCE 6
ANGEL V
By Anthony Fields

A THUGS STREET PRINCESS 3
By Meesha

CORNER BOYS 2
By Corey Robinson

THA TAKEOVER
By Keith Chandler

BETRAYAL OF A G 2
By Ray Vinci

SAVAGE FAMILY EMPIRE 1&2
SOULLESS GOON 1,2&3
THE DIRTY SIDE OF MONEY 1,2&3
By Prince

FOR MY ENEMY'S SAKE
AMBITIONS OF A SLIDER
FRESH OFF DA PORCH
By IRA B.

THE TRUCKLOAD 1-4
TIPPIN' THE SCALES 1-3
BAD BITCHES WIT GUNZ 3
PROBLEM SOLVED 2
By Christopher "Diesel" Hornezes

Available Now

RESTRAINING ORDER 1 & 2
By **CA$H & Coffee**

LOVE KNOWS NO BOUNDARIES 1-3
By **Coffee**

RAISED AS A GOON I, II, III & IV
BRED BY THE SLUMS I, II, III
BLAST FOR ME I & II
ROTTEN TO THE CORE I II III
A BRONX TALE I, II, III
DUFFLE BAG CARTEL I II III IV V VI
HEARTLESS GOON I II III IV V
A SAVAGE DOPEBOY I II
DRUG LORDS I II III
CUTTHROAT MAFIA I II
KING OF THE TRENCHES
By **Ghost**

LAY IT DOWN I & II
LAST OF A DYING BREED I II
BLOOD STAINS OF A SHOTTA I & II III
By **Jamaica**

LOYAL TO THE GAME I II III
LIFE OF SIN I, II III
By **TJ & Jelissa**

IF LOVING HIM IS WRONG…I & II
LOVE ME EVEN WHEN IT HURTS I II III
By **Jelissa**

PUSH IT TO THE LIMIT
By **Bre' Hayes**

BLOODY COMMAS I & II
SKI MASK CARTEL I, II & III
KING OF NEW YORK I II, III IV V
RISE TO POWER I II III
COKE KINGS I II III IV V
BORN HEARTLESS I II III IV
KING OF THE TRAP I II
By **T.J. Edwards**

WHEN THE STREETS CLAP BACK I & II III
THE HEART OF A SAVAGE I II III IV
MONEY MAFIA I II
LOYAL TO THE SOIL I II III
By **Jibril Williams**

A DISTINGUISHED THUG STOLE MY HEART I II & III
LOVE SHOULDN'T HURT I II III IV
RENEGADE BOYS 1-4
PAID IN KARMA 1-3
SAVAGE STORMS 1-3
AN UNFORESEEN LOVE 1-3
BABY, I'M WINTERTIME COLD 1-3
A THUG'S STREET PRINCESS 1&2
By **Meesha**

A GANGSTER'S CODE 1-3
A GANGSTER'S SYN 1-3
THE SAVAGE LIFE 1-3
CHAINED TO THE STREETS 1-3
BLOOD ON THE MONEY 1-3
A GANGSTA'S PAIN 1-3
BEAUTIFUL LIES AND UGLY TRUTHS
CHURCH IN THESE STREETS
By **J-Blunt**

CUM FOR ME 1-8
An LDP Erotica Collaboration

THA TAKEOVER | KEITH CHANDLER JR.

BLOOD OF A BOSS 1-5
SHADOWS OF THE GAME
TRAP BASTARD
By **Askari**

THE STREETS BLEED MURDER 1-3
THE HEART OF A GANGSTA 1-3
By **Jerry Jackson**

WHEN A GOOD GIRL GOES BAD
By **Adrienne**

THE COST OF LOYALTY 1-3
By **Kweli**

BRIDE OF A HUSTLA 1-3
THE FETTI GIRLS 1-3
CORRUPTED BY A GANGSTA 1-4
BLINDED BY HIS LOVE
THE PRICE YOU PAY FOR LOVE 1-3
DOPE GIRL MAGIC 1-3
By **Destiny Skai**

A KINGPIN'S AMBITION
A KINGPIN'S AMBITION II
I MURDER FOR THE DOUGH
By **Ambitious**

TRUE SAVAGE 1-7
DOPE BOY MAGIC 1-3
MIDNIGHT CARTEL 1-3
CITY OF KINGZ 1&2
NIGHTMARE ON SILENT AVE
THE PLUG OF LIL MEXICO 1&2
CLASSIC CITY
By **Chris Green**

THA TAKEOVER | KEITH CHANDLER JR.

A GANGSTER'S REVENGE 1-4
THE BOSS MAN'S DAUGHTERS 1-5
A SAVAGE LOVE 1&2
BAE BELONGS TO ME 1&2
A HUSTLER'S DECEIT 1-3
WHAT BAD BITCHES DO 1-3
SOUL OF A MONSTER 1-3
KILL ZONE
A DOPE BOY'S QUEEN 1-3
TIL DEATH 1-3
IMMA DIE BOUT MINE 1-6
DYING FOR LIKES
By **Aryanna**

A DOPEBOY'S PRAYER
By **Eddie "Wolf" Lee**

THE KING CARTEL 1-3
By **Frank Gresham**

THESE NIGGAS AIN'T LOYAL 1-3
By **Nikki Tee**

GANGSTA SHYT 1-3
By **CATO**

THE ULTIMATE BETRAYAL
By **Phoenix**

BOSS'N UP 1-3
By **Royal Nicole**

I LOVE YOU TO DEATH
By **Destiny J**

I RIDE FOR MY HITTA
I STILL RIDE FOR MY HITTA
By **Misty Holt**

LOVE & CHASIN' PAPER
By **Qay Crockett**

TO DIE IN VAIN
SINS OF A HUSTLA
By **ASAD**

BROOKLYN HUSTLAZ
By **Boogsy Morina**

BROOKLYN ON LOCK 1 & 2
By **Sonovia**

GANGSTA CITY
By **Teddy Duke**

A DRUG KING AND HIS DIAMOND 1-3
A DOPEMAN'S RICHES
HER MAN, MINE'S TOO 1&2
CASH MONEY HO'S
THE WIFEY I USED TO BE 1&2
PRETTY GIRLS DO NASTY THINGS
By **Nicole Goosby**

LIPSTICK KILLAH 1-3
CRIME OF PASSION 1-3
FRIEND OR FOE 1-3
By **Mimi**

TRAPHOUSE KING 1-3
KINGPIN KILLAZ 1-3
STREET KINGS 1&2
PAID IN BLOOD 1&2
CARTEL KILLAZ 1-3
DOPE GODS 1&2
By **Hood Rich**

THE STREETS ARE CALLING
By **Duquie Wilson**

STEADY MOBBN' 1-3
THE STREETS STAINED MY SOUL 1-3
By **Marcellus Allen**

WHO SHOT YA 1-3
SON OF A DOPE FIEND 1-4
HEAVEN GOT A GHETTO 1&2
SKI MASK MONEY 1&2
By **Renta**

GORILLAZ IN THE BAY 1-4
TEARS OF A GANGSTA 1/&2
3X KRAZY 1&2
STRAIGHT BEAST MODE 1&2
By **DE'KARI**

TRIGGADALE 1-3
MURDA WAS THE CASE 1-3
By **Elijah R. Freeman**

SLAUGHTER GANG 1-3
RUTHLESS HEART 1-3
By **Willie Slaughter**

GOD BLESS THE TRAPPERS 1-3
THESE SCANDALOUS STREETS 1-3
FEAR MY GANGSTA 1-5
THESE STREETS DON'T LOVE NOBODY 1-2
BURY ME A G 1-5
A GANGSTA'S EMPIRE 1-4
THE DOPEMAN'S BODYGAURD 1&2
THE REALEST KILLAZ 1-3
THE LAST OF THE OGS 1-3
By **Tranay Adams**

MARRIED TO A BOSS 1-3
By **Destiny Skai & Chris Green**

KINGZ OF THE GAME 1-7
CRIME BOSS 1-4
By **Playa Ray**

FUK SHYT
By **Blakk Diamond**

DON'T F#CK WITH MY HEART 1&2
By **Linnea**

ADDICTED TO THE DRAMA 1-3
IN THE ARM OF HIS BOSS
By **Jamila**

LOYALTY AIN'T PROMISED 1&2
By **Keith Williams**

YAYO 1-4
A SHOOTER'S AMBITION 1&2
BRED IN THE GAME
By **S. Allen**

TRAP GOD 1-3
RICH $AVAGE 1-3
MONEY IN THE GRAVE 1-3
CARTEL MONEY 1&2
By **Martell Troublesome Bolden**

FOREVER GANGSTA 1&2
GLOCKS ON SATIN SHEETS 1&2
By **Adrian Dulan**

TOE TAGZ 1-4
LEVELS TO THIS SHYT 1&2
IT'S JUST ME AND YOU
By **Ah'Million**

KINGPIN DREAMS 1-3
RAN OFF ON DA PLUG
By **Paper Boi Rari**

THE STREETS MADE ME 1-3
By **Larry D. Wright**

CONFESSIONS OF A GANGSTA 1-4
CONFESSIONS OF A JACKBOY 1-3
CONFESSIONS OF A HITMAN
CONFESSIONS OF A DOPE BOY
By **Nicholas Lock**

I'M NOTHING WITHOUT HIS LOVE
SINS OF A THUG
TO THE THUG I LOVED BEFORE
A GANGSTA SAVED XMAS
IN A HUSTLER I TRUST
By **Monet Dragun**

QUIET MONEY 1-3
THUG LIFE 1-3
EXTENDED CLIP 1&2
A GANGSTA'S PARADISE
By **Trai'Quan**

CAUGHT UP IN THE LIFE 1-3
THE STREETS NEVER LET GO 1-3
By **Robert Baptiste**

NEW TO THE GAME 1-3
MONEY, MURDER & MEMORIES 1-3
By **Malik D. Rice**

CREAM 2-3
THE STREETS WILL TALK
By **Yolanda Moore**

THE STREETS WILL NEVER CLOSE 1-3
By **K'ajji**

LIFE OF A SAVAGE 1-4
A GANGSTA'S QUR'AN 1-4
MURDA SEASON 1-3
GANGLAND CARTEL 1-3
CHI'RAQ GANGSTAS 1-4
KILLERS ON ELM STREET 1-3
JACK BOYZ N DA BRONX 1-3
A DOPEBOY'S DREAM 1-3
JACK BOYS VS DOPE BOYS 1-3
COKE GIRLZ
COKE BOYS
SOSA GANG 1&2
BRONX SAVAGES
BODYMORE KINGPINS
BLOOD OF A GOON
By **Romell Tukes**

CONCRETE KILLA 1-3
VICIOUS LOYALTY 1-3
BLOODY MONEY BAGS
By **Kingpen**

THE ULTIMATE SACRIFICE 1-6
KHADIFI
IF YOU CROSS ME ONCE 1-3
ANGEL 1-4
IN THE BLINK OF AN EYE
By **Anthony Fields**

THE LIFE OF A HOOD STAR
By **Ca$h & Rashia Wilson**

NIGHTMARES OF A HUSTLA 1-3
BLOOD AND GAMES 1&2
By **King Dream**

GHOST MOB
By **Stilloan Robinson**

HARD AND RUTHLESS 1&2
MOB TOWN 251
THE BILLIONAIRE BENTLEYS 1-3
REAL G'S MOVE IN SILENCE
By **Von Diesel**

MOB TIES 1-7
SOUL OF A HUSTLER, HEART OF A KILLER 1-3
GORILLAZ IN THE TRENCHES
OOPS CRY TOO 1&2
THE DAUGHTER OF A CARTEL BOSS
By **SayNoMore**

BODYMORE MURDERLAND 1-3
THE BIRTH OF A GANGSTER 1-4
By **Delmont Player**

FOR THE LOVE OF A BOSS 1&2
By **C. D. Blue**

KILLA KOUNTY 1-5
TENDER
By **Khufu**

MOBBED UP 1-4
THE BRICK MAN 1-5
THE COCAINE PRINCESS 1-10
STEPPERS 1-3
SUPER GREMLIN 1-4
A GANGSTA'S SON
By **King Rio**

MONEY GAME 1&2
By **Smoove Dolla**

A GANGSTA'S KARMA 1-5
By **FLAME**

KING OF THE TRENCHES 1-3
By **GHOST & TRANAY ADAMS**

BAD BITCHES WIT GUNZ 1&2
PROBLEM SOLVED
By **"Christopher Diesel" Hornezes**

QUEEN OF THE ZOO 1&2
By **Black Migo**

GRIMEY WAYS 1-3
BETRAYAL OF A G
By **Ray Vinci**

XMAS WITH AN ATL SHOOTER
By **Ca$h & Destiny Skai**

KING KILLA 1&2
By **Vincent "Vitto" Holloway**

BETRAYAL OF A THUG 1&2
By **Fre$h**

COUNTDOWN OF A KILLA 1&2
SEX, MURDER AND GOD 1&2
GUNS DOWN, BOTTOMS UP 1&2
By Lo-Life

THE MURDER QUEENS 1-7
By **Michael Gallon**

FOR THE LOVE OF BLOOD 1-4
By **Jamel Mitchell**

THA TAKEOVER | KEITH CHANDLER JR.

HOOD CONSIGLIERE 1&2
NO TIME FOR ERROR
By **Keese**

PROTÉGÉ OF A LEGEND 1,2&3
LOVE IN THE TRENCHES 1&2
By **Corey Robinson**

THE PLUG'S RUTHLESS DAUGHTER 1&2
By **Tony Daniels**

BORN IN THE GRAVE 1-3
CRIME PAYS
By **Self Made Tay**

MOAN IN MY MOUTH
By **XTASY**

TORN BETWEEN A GANGSTER AND A GENTLEMAN
By **J-BLUNT & Miss Kim**

LOYALTY IS EVERYTHING 1-3
CITY OF SMOKE 1-3
By **Molotti**

HERE TODAY GONE TOMORROW 1&2
By **Fly Rock**

WOMEN LIE MEN LIE 1-4
FIFTY SHADES OF SNOW 1-3
STACK BEFORE YOU SPLURGE
GIRLS FALL LIKE DOMINOES
NAÏVE TO THE STREETS
By **ROY MILLIGAN**

PILLOW PRINCESS
By **S. Hawkins**

THE BUTTERFLY MAFIA 1-3
SALUTE MY SAVAGERY 1&2
By **Fumiya Payne**

THE LANE 1&2
By Ken-Ken Spence

THE PUSSY TRAP 1-5
By **Nene Capri**

DIRTY DNA
By **Blaque**

SANCTIFIED AND HORNY
by **XTASY**

BOOKS BY LDP'S CEO, CA$H

TRUST IN NO MAN
TRUST IN NO MAN 2
TRUST IN NO MAN 3
BONDED BY BLOOD
SHORTY GOT A THUG
THUGS CRY
THUGS CRY 2
THUGS CRY 3
TRUST NO BITCH
TRUST NO BITCH 2
TRUST NO BITCH 3
TIL MY CASKET DROPS
RESTRAINING ORDER
RESTRAINING ORDER 2
IN LOVE WITH A CONVICT
LIFE OF A HOOD STAR
XMAS WITH AN ATL SHOOTER